D0940420

DEATH IN A STATELY HOME

DEATH IN A STATELY HOME

BOOK THREE IN THE MURDER ON LOCATION SERIES

SARA ROSETT

McGuffin Ink

DEATH IN A STATELY HOME
Book Three in the *Murder on Location* series
An English Village Murder Mystery
Published by McGuffin Ink

Copyright © 2015 by Sara Rosett
Second Paperback Edition: October 2016
First Paperback Edition: October 2015
ISBN: 978-0-9982535-2-7
Cover Design: James at GoOnWrite.com

All rights are reserved. Without limiting the rights under copyright reserved
above, no part of this work may be used, stored, transmitted, or reproduced in any
manner or form whatsoever without express written permission from the author
and publisher.

This is a work of fiction and names, characters, incidents, and places are products
of the author's imagination or used fictitiously. Any resemblance to persons, living
or dead, incidents, and places is coincidental.

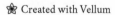 Created with Vellum

ABOUT DEATH IN A STATELY HOME

Good houseguests don't get accused of murder...

Kate Sharp loves the perks of her location scout profession. When she fills in for a researcher at a Regency-themed English house party, she's looking forward to indulging in the posh atmosphere of tea on the lawn and elegant candlelight dinners, but when a guest is murdered in a locked room, Kate becomes the prime suspect.

As she turns her attention to the guests, the staff, and the owners, Kate must unlock the mystery and uncover the murderer before she's arrested for a crime she didn't commit.

Death in a Stately Home is the third installment in the *Murder on Location* collection, a series of British cozy mysteries. If you love engaging characters, compelling British detective mysteries, the works of Jane Austen, and vivid locations that transport you to another place, then you'll love Sara Rosett's latest whodunit.

SCHEDULE OF EVENTS

Parkview Hall

Schedule of Activities

Friday
4:30 ~ Tea on the Small Terrace
7:00 ~ Drinks in the Drawing Room
7:30 ~ Dinner

Saturday
7:00 to 10:00 ~ Breakfast
Tray in your room or join us in the Breakfast Room
Morning at your leisure
Noon ~ Cold luncheon served on the Small Terrace
Afternoon ~ your choice of activities
Regency needlework lesson
Clay pigeon shooting
Boating on the lake
Garden and greenhouse tour
4:30 ~ Tea in your room or as requested during activities

7:00 ~ Drinks in the Drawing Room
7:30 ~ Dinner

Sunday
7:00 to 10:00 ~ Breakfast
Tray in your room or join us in the Breakfast Room
Morning at your leisure
11:00 ~ Departure

"Selfishness must always be forgiven you know, because there is no hope of a cure."
—Jane Austen, *Mansfield Park*

CHAPTER 1

$\mathscr{B}$EATRICE'S CRISP UPPER-CLASS ACCENT had a worried undertone, which was not like her at all. "Kate," she said as I listened to her voice message, "I have a spot of bother that I'd like to speak to you about. A rather delicate situation. Can you ring me back as soon as possible? The country house party begins today, and I must talk with you before then. It's quite urgent."

Beatrice—whose formal title was Lady Stone of Parkview Hall, the local country pile that drew tourists from miles around —was straightforward and matter-of-fact. Evasive wasn't her style. I frowned and called her back, keeping one eye out for a lumbering double-decker bus making its way to the village green. When I was put through to the estate office at Parkview Hall, I was told Beatrice had stepped out.

"Any message?" asked a helpful voice.

"No. I'll call back in a moment."

I hung up and turned to Alex to tell him about the message, but his head was bent over his phone, reading a text. "Grace says she is almost here."

I put the unease about Beatrice's message on hold and

switched to the bigger concern that I'd been thinking about all day. "That's…great."

Alex's fingers stilled. "You sound worried."

I sighed. What had been a tiny doubt last week, had increased to full-blown worry as Grace's visit neared. Standing in the warm summer sunshine, I couldn't ignore it anymore. "Okay, yes, I am. I think I should go home."

"Why?" Alex asked, his face perplexed.

"Because you said that when you told Grace that I'd be here, she just said 'okay.'"

"What's wrong with that?"

"Grace is coming home to see you, not you *and* me. She doesn't even know me. You should spend some time with her before you spring me on her. I mean, what schoolgirl on holiday wants to have a stranger horning in on her time with her brother?"

"Don't stress. Grace is awesome. She's always grumbling about me being so much older and a boy, to boot. She'll be thrilled that you're here."

"Hmm."

Alex slipped his phone into his pocket and turned toward me, using his shoulder to separate us from the group milling around Nether Woodsmoor's green as they waited for the bus. "And I'm not springing you on her. She knows about you. Like I said, I've told her about you. You're part of my life now. I want her to get to know you."

He smiled that special smile that made my insides melt a little. Normally, I was all about losing myself in that smile, but I squeezed his hand and resisted the power of his smile. "What *exactly* did she say when you told her about me, that I'd be here during her half term break?"

"She said 'okay.'"

"And that was it?"

"Yes. She's fine with it."

2

"Alex," I patted his arm. "You are so sweet. You're usually so intuitive about women, but I don't think you have a clue about twelve-year-old girls. One-word responses are not good. Not good at all."

Alex frowned. "You think so?"

"Yes. Twelve is the age when girls can't stop talking...unless they're in a mood, and then you can't get them to say a word."

"How do you know this?"

"I was a twelve-year-old once. Listen, I'll head back to my cottage. You two go on the picnic. I'll meet her tomorrow—" I broke off as the bus came into view. I spotted a girl with long dark hair in the front seat of the top deck, her round face hovering near the window like a balloon. Our gazes connected, then she spotted Alex and waved, her face breaking into a grin.

I couldn't leave now. "Or...I'll just stay here and meet her."

The bus circled the roundabout laboriously like a tired circus elephant performing in the ring and shuddered to a stop. With a hydraulic wheeze, the driver lowered the bus. Despite being on the top deck, Grace was one of the first riders off the bus. She dodged through the line of people waiting to get on the bus and made for Alex, the plaid skirt of her uniform fluttering. Alex swept her up in a hug that lifted her off her feet.

I stood back while they greeted each other, looking on with the other strangers around the bus, most of whom smiled as they watched the reunion. My phone in my pocket buzzed, and I checked it quickly. It was Elise, the producer of the Jane Austen documentary. Both Alex and I worked for her. She wasn't a woman who liked to leave messages, but I couldn't take her call now. I pressed the button to send the call to voicemail, wondering uneasily why she had called. The whole production had the weekend off.

Alex set Grace on her feet and stepped back. "Grown another inch, I see."

"Two centimeters." Grace wore a white short-sleeved shirt

with her plaid skirt. Navy knee socks and dark shoes completed the outfit. She held a navy blazer balled up under one arm. "We're in the U.K., remember? That's what Mrs. Maslan keeps telling me," she said with a roll of her eyes. "We use the metric system here," she repeated in a singsong voice. "Anyway," she said, returning to her normal tones, "I'm one hundred sixty centimeters." Like me, both Alex and Grace were American transplants to England.

Alex squinted up at the church's steeple that soared over the green. "So, in feet and inches....?"

"Five-three," she replied instantly.

"Thank you. Now I don't have to Google it. I bet you didn't have to look it up."

"No, it's a simple formula."

Alex draped his arm around Grace and said to me. "Her favorite subject is math."

"Maths, you mean." Grace gave a little shake of her head, conveying loving exasperation with her brother.

"Kate, this is Grace," Alex said, shifting so that they were facing me. "Grace, my good friend Kate."

"Hi, Grace. Amazing how many little differences there are between American English and British English," I said, latching onto the subject, hoping to find a little common ground with her.

"Yes, like torch. The girls kept talking about torches, and I really wanted one until I found out it was just a stupid flashlight." Her gaze ran over me from head to toe, then she asked, "Are you Alex's *girlfriend* or just a *friend*?" She gazed expectantly at me with the same dark chocolate eyes as her brother.

I looked at Alex over her head. "I think you could say I'm his girlfriend." No formal declarations had been made, but we were certainly a couple.

Alex smiled back at me with an intense gaze, and I felt like I was the most important thing in the world to him, his only focus at the moment. "Definitely."

"Oh," Grace said in a small voice.

I dragged my gaze away from Alex and realized that Grace had turned and was glancing back and forth from Alex to me. I redirected my attention to her, but she whirled around and called, "Suitcase," as she disappeared back through the line of people now inching into the bus.

When she and Alex returned with her suitcase, Grace announced, "I'm starving," and looked over at the White Duck pub. Alex hitched his backpack, which was slung over one shoulder, higher. "Picnic lunch. Where would you like to go? The river or the green? Or we could drop your suitcase at the cottage and go up to the ruins, if you feel like a hike."

Grace scanned the street. "Is your car not fixed?"

"No, it's repaired." Alex said.

Alex's classic MG Midget convertible had been damaged and was in the repair shop for a while, but it was functioning again.

"Then why didn't you bring it?" Grace asked.

"We couldn't all fit in it for one thing."

Grace shot me a look from under her lashes, and I knew she was thinking that if there were only two of them, it would have been fine—plenty of room. "You brought it last time."

"It was pouring rain. Today is a gorgeous day. So river or green?" Alex asked again.

It was the sort of day that inspired poets to wax lyrical about the English countryside. A cloudless, brilliantly blue sky contrasted with the varying greens of the trees. A profusion of flowers from palest pink roses to tall bright yellow sunflowers filled the gardens around the green. A light breeze made the delicate petals dance and the sunflowers bob.

"River, I guess."

A faint sulky undertone slipped into Grace's voice, which I heard loud and clear. My unease grew as we walked the short distance to the river with Grace between Alex and me.

Alex took Grace's suitcase handle and pulled it along. "So how was the trip here?" He asked as we turned down one of the village streets lined with shops and restaurants, each with bright flowers trailing from hanging baskets or window boxes. The summer influx of cyclists and grand home touring families were out in force this weekend. Under awnings that breathed like living things in the gentle breeze, every chair at the sidewalk cafés were full, and we had to dodge through a crowd of milling tourists.

Grace shifted around to the other side of Alex. "Fine."

We emerged into the open paved area that ran along the flat, but fast-moving river. All the benches were full, and people were strolling by the water, but Alex pointed to an open patch of ground near one of the bridges where the river curved.

He claimed the section of open space, and didn't seem to notice that Grace had slowed and was now several steps behind us. Alex parked the suitcase near the bridge, then I helped him spread the blanket he'd brought. I sat down on a corner, and Alex dropped down beside me. Grace stood a moment, then settled across from us, her back to the river.

"Ham or turkey?" Alex asked.

Grace shrugged.

"Ham, it is." Alex handed her the sandwich, then distributed the rest of the food and drinks. Alex was so easy-going that it took a lot to ruffle his feathers, but I saw him send a frowning look toward Grace, and I knew he wasn't happy with her attitude.

Grace devoured her sandwich, then finished off an apple and a large cookie. I exchanged a grin with Alex as Grace rummaged in the backpack for the bag of chips—or crisps, as she called them. Maybe the girl was just cranky and hungry. She sat with her head down, her dark hair falling forward, hiding her face.

We ate, the steady hum of the water rushing along under the bridge, the only sound except for stray bits of conversation that floated our way from people walking along the river or over the bridge.

A woman with faded brown hair made her way toward the bridge. She wore a saggy white tunic-type shirt over a pair of loose pants that flared around her ankles. I shifted, preparing to stand.

"See someone?" Alex asked.

I saw the woman's face and relaxed. "No. I thought I saw Beatrice, but it wasn't her." I reached for a chip. "She called and left me a message. I returned her call, but she wasn't in. She sounded....worried."

"Who's Beatrice?" Grace asked.

"Lady Stone," Alex explained. "She and her husband Sir Harold live in Parkview Hall, the big estate we toured last time you were here."

"Oh. The one with all the chairs roped off."

"She sounded worried?" Alex asked. "That doesn't sound like her."

"I know. She had said she needed my help with 'a spot of bother,' as she phrased it." Beatrice was not a person who spent time worrying over things. She was much more of the let's-get-this-thing-taken-care-of school of thought. She didn't mull things over. She organized, sorted, and dealt with problems, neatly slotting them into proper categories.

"I'm sure she'll call you back," Alex said.

"Oh, I don't doubt it." Beatrice was also very determined and focused. Once you were on her agenda, you might as well surrender to her plans. "She did mention this weekend's house party. I hope nothing has gone wrong."

"If it has, I'm sure she'll fix it in no time." Alex balled up the napkins and chip bags as he asked Grace, "So what would you like to do today? Should we go to the ruins this afternoon?"

"I'd rather slackline instead."

"Slackline? What's that?" I asked.

Alex eyed Grace as he answered. "It's sort of like walking a tightrope, but you use a flat, webbed line."

"I knew you'd know about it," Grace said, her voice animated again.

Before Alex had taken up location scouting, he'd been heavily into extreme sports, his favorite being snowboarding. "Like up in the air?" I asked.

"Yes," Grace said, unperturbed. "But you don't start high, only a few feet off the ground." She shifted her attention to Alex. "So you've done it, right?"

"I tried it, but I wasn't into it. Where did you learn about slacklining?" Alex asked, in a rather parental tone.

"We did it at Marie's house when I went home with her over the weekend. Her brother had one set up, and he let us use it. You've got some tie-downs," Grace said. "I saw them in the cupboard last time I was here. We could put them up between the two trees in the back garden—"

"Not today," Alex said. "We're going to the ruins, while the weather is nice."

Grace shut down, the animation draining from her face. "Are you coming, Kate?"

"Of course Kate is coming." Alex reached out to take my hand. "Kate loves the hike to the ruins."

"I do," I said. "It's one of my favorite walks."

"Right." Grace said so softly that I almost couldn't hear her. Her gaze lingered on our linked hands. Abruptly, she asked, "Do you know how to french braid hair?"

"Um...no, not french braid. I can do a regular braid though."

"That's okay," Grace said, but I had a feeling that it wasn't okay at all.

We tossed the last of the crumbs to the ducks, then packed up the blanket and made our way back through Nether Woodsmoor to the steep street that branched off one of the main roads. We traipsed up the street, and I was glad it was Alex pulling Grace's large suitcase up the incline, not me. When we reached Cottage Lane, I looked over my shoulder at Grace, who was lagging several paces behind us, trailing her hand along the stacked stone wall that formed the front of each cottage garden. The heady fragrances of flowers from the front gardens wafted over us as we walked. I exchanged a glance with Alex. He shrugged and mouthed the word *sorry*.

"It's fine," I said softly as we reached the gate that opened into the garden in front of my cottage. "Well, this is me." I stepped through and noticed a bit of the tension in Grace's shoulders ease. "I'll give you time to settle in. Why don't you two go on to the ruins this afternoon without me," I said to Alex.

"You don't have to—"

"No, Grace needs to unpack, and Elise called a little while ago. I should call her back." After a rocky start, my boss and I had reached an uneasy truce. I didn't want a resumption of the hostilities. I'd already sent her call to voicemail. The sooner I called her back, the better. "And I still have to track down Beatrice. I need to take care of those things," I said quickly because I could see that Alex was about to protest again. I squeezed his hand. "Really, it's okay. I think you two should go on."

Grace moved around Alex, her steps quickening. "Bye, Kate."

"If you're sure..." Alex said.

"Yes. Positive."

"Okay, but you're not skipping out of pizza tonight."

"Wouldn't dream of it."

Alex planted a quick kiss on my mouth. "See you soon," he said quietly.

Grace reached the end of the lane. She gave me a long solemn look as she turned into the gate at Alex's cottage.

I CLOSED the door and leaned on it, blowing out a long breath. "Well, that didn't go as planned." I looked around my little cottage with its hardwood floors and the strange modern furniture left by a prior tenant that didn't go with the cozy atmosphere of wooden beams and bookcases on either side of the fireplace. During the rather cool and rainy spring, I'd often sat on the uncomfortable angular couch beside the fireplace, reading and preparing my location scouting reports, but now in the heat of summer, the room was stifling.

I opened the window that looked out over the front garden, heaving up the casement with its wavy glass, then I moved down the little hallway that ran from the front door to the kitchen at the back of the cottage. In the kitchen I propped open the back door.

I returned to the front room and stood still, testing the air. Yes, the air shifted slightly, feathering along my skin. I made a mental note to buy a fan. The last few days had been incredibly hot—boiling, as my friend Louise described it—compared to the mild summer weather we'd been having. While the day felt pleasant when you were outside, indoors was a different story. The bright sun beat down on the cottage, and with its poor circulation, the temperature only went up as the day went on. Coming from Southern California, where air conditioning was practically a basic human right, the fact that the cottage didn't have at least a window cooler was a shock.

I dialed Elise's number as I walked out to the back garden. Elise answered on the first ring. "Kate. I called you over thirty minutes ago."

I gritted my teeth. "Hello, Elise," I said deliberately. Most of the Brits I met were extremely polite, but Elise didn't believe in chit-chat—or greetings. "This is the first opportunity I've had to call you back. We're not working this weekend, you know."

"And look at this weather. Gorgeous. So annoying that we're not in a position to get any of it on film. I can't believe I let Paul talk me into a break in filming. Next time, we're going straight through."

I dropped into one of two plastic chairs positioned in the shade of an oak tree.

"But wasn't there a conflict with the talent?" It wouldn't do us any good to film if we didn't have our actors in place to portray the scenes we needed to film.

"Actors can be replaced," Elise said airily. "We could film from a distance and get the closeups later. Kate, you're in Nether Woodsmoor?" she said abruptly.

"Yes," I said slowly with a sense of unease. Elise's conversational shifts often left me disoriented, but I knew I didn't want Elise tracking my movements. She wasn't the sort of person you wanted to know your whereabouts.

"Good. Marion is on bedrest. I need you to go to Parkview Hall."

"I can run by there today," I said, feeling relieved. A short errand was easy. "What do you need? And is Marion okay?" Marion was the production's researcher. She was five months pregnant with her first child.

"She's fine, except she has to stay off her feet so the weekend house party is out of the question. That's why I need you to go. Notes, background, the whole bit. We don't need photos. We're familiar enough with the Hall."

Elise had a tendency to move at the speed of light. "Weekend house party?" I asked to slow her down.

"Regency-themed. Tea on the lawn. Dressing for dinner. Shooting and riding, too, I suppose, if you go in for that sort of thing. All without hoards of tourists breathing down your neck."

"Okay, yes, Beatrice mentioned it." I'd seen the brochure for it during one of our shoots at Parkview Hall.

"With Marion out of commission, I need someone there to assess it for inclusion in the production." Elise spaced her words out as if she was speaking to a simpleton.

"And you want me to do that? I'm not a researcher. I don't know what Marion does."

"It's similar to location scouting." Impatience tinged Elise's words. "Take notes on the events. Write up a summary report with potential uses of the event. Can we use it for B-roll? Or would there be enough there for a *Jane in the Modern World* feature?"

The documentary series was an in-depth look at Austen's life. So far, episodes had featured reenactments of scenes from some of Austen's novels as well as reenactments of Austen's life. Short features were interspersed with commentary from experts. The features had explored Jane Austen and pop culture as well as life in Regency times.

"Beatrice informs me that they will hold at least two more house party weekends this summer. I need to know right away so we can book one of the remaining two, if it will be a feasible use of our time. Lady Stone has comped one guest for the weekend, so we can't let it go to waste. You're the closest. You can be there tonight."

I clamped my lips together to keep from uttering the protests that were welling up. Of course, a house party at Parkview Hall would normally be at the top of my list of things I'd love to do. In fact, I'd seen the brochure and thought wistfully that I would like to go, but the hefty price tag put it far—extremely far—out of my budget. Exclusive country home weekends didn't come cheap, and there was no way I could afford one on my location scout salary. And I bet Parkview Hall with its stone exterior, huge corridors, and vaulted ceilings would be delightfully cool, much cooler than my stuffy bedroom under the cottage eaves. I'd spent a restless night last night tossing and turning and wishing I'd saved enough money to buy a window air conditioning unit.

But despite loving the idea of attending a real English country house party, the fact remained that I had plans with Alex this weekend. Just because I lived close to Parkview Hall didn't mean that Elise could draft me with only a few hours notice to step into a job that I didn't know. But that was Elise in a nutshell. I suspected that she thought of everyone who worked for her as interchangeable cogs and that each of us only existed to further her goals.

My extended silence must have clued her in that I wasn't jumping up and down at the opportunity. "Kate, this is a once in a lifetime opportunity."

"True, but I already have plans for this weekend."

After a few moments of silence on her end of the line, she cleared her throat. "Really. I hadn't thought it would be a problem. You can't rearrange things? It *is* Parkview Hall, and I know how interested you are in all things Regency. Surely you don't want to pass up a chance to live like a Regency miss for a weekend?"

"Well...it does sound intriguing."

"You don't have to stay at Parkview continuously," Elise said, sensing a weak point. "You'd be free to come and go as you like. All I need is an overview. Once you have the gist what is going on, you could enjoy the party or leave. As long as you get the high points for me, that is." Sounding as if it physically pained her, she added, "And it would be overtime, of course."

"I might be able to shift a few things around," I said, thinking that my first interactions with Grace hadn't been that promising. It might be better to back off and give her and Alex most of the weekend together. I could drop in a couple of times to see them... and possibly get that window air conditioning unit, too.

"Excellent," Elise said briskly.

"Wait," I said quickly, a thought striking me. "What is my position?"

"Position?"

"At the house party? I'm not a chambermaid or poor relation or something like that?" I remembered from the brochure that guests would have definite roles over the weekend. We were a budget production, and I wouldn't put it beyond Elise to send someone to the house party in the lowest social position possible.

"No, of course not. You couldn't ask someone to pay for the weekend then expect them to polish the furniture and lay the fires," Elise said, but I heard a rustling of papers. "Yes, here it is. Guest level: gentry. Historically appropriate clothing provided. All meals and entertainment included."

I felt a flutter of excitement. It *was* a once in a lifetime opportunity, and I thought Alex would understand. It involved one of Elise's commands, which were frequent. He knew how imperious she could be, and both our jobs depended on staying in her good graces. With the flexibility to come and go as I liked, it should be a fun weekend. "I think I could do that."

"Excellent. Arrival before five."

CHAPTER 2

*A*FTER I ENDED THE CALL with Elise, I called Parkview Hall and reached Beatrice. "Kate, Thank you for ringing back. You're coming in Marion's place, I understand."

"Yes, I just got off the phone with Elise."

"Excellent. This will work out better than I'd planned. I'd hoped to slip you onto the guest list surreptitiously, but this will be so much better. You'll be here soon?"

"Yes, as soon as I speak to Alex. I have to juggle some plans for the weekend."

"Oh, I'm sorry. Would Alex like to attend as well?"

While the idea of Alex turned out in a Regency coat and breeches appealed to me, I doubted that it was his idea of a good time. Since he avoided wearing even a sport coat, he'd probably run as fast as he could from starched cravats. "No, his sister is in town. I think they need some time on their own. This will work out fine."

"They're welcome to drop in for tea. Just let Waverly know."

"Waverly?"

"Our butler."

"I didn't realize you had a butler." I knew Beatrice employed a housekeeper and a skeleton staff to cook and clean for her and Sir Harold as well as several people who helped her run the stately home when it was open to the public. The only other staff I'd seen when I visited Parkview Hall were tour guides shepherding tourists.

"Only for events like the house party or weddings and such. He comes with the caterer, you know," Beatrice said with a laugh. "Frightfully correct and dull. My goal this weekend is to make him crack a smile. Now. Where were we? When you arrive, tell Waverly who you are, and he'll bring you to me directly." Her voice sobered. "I have certain...issues... I'd like to discuss with you in private."

I ended the call, more worried than ever. Beatrice had again sounded apprehensive, even a bit fearful. In short, not like herself at all.

~

"It's just going to take a little time," Alex said quietly as he swept up playing pieces from the board game Cluedo, which I recognized as the British version of Clue, a game I'd loved as a kid—another of those similar, yet different things between the U.S. and the U.K.

"I know," I replied in the same soft undertone. "That's why I agreed to go to Parkview Hall. It will give you and Grace time together. She needs that. I think it was a little too much, too fast for her this afternoon."

There was no need for us to speak so quietly. We stood in Alex's kitchen near a fan that swiveled back and forth, but only stirred up the warm air inside his cottage. The sound of pop music pulsed down the hall from behind Grace's closed bedroom door, doing an effective job of drowning out our words.

"She used to love this game." Alex dropped the playing pieces into the slot in the box. "Last time she was home, we played it so many times I was sick of Professor Plum and Colonel Mustard. She barely glanced at it when she came in today. She said she wanted to polish her nails. She's not even excited about going to the ruins later today. She's always liked climbing over the walls."

"It all sounds completely normal to me. She's growing up. She probably thinks board games are for kids and that she's too old to climb walls now. She's almost a teenager. "

Alex groaned. "Let's not even talk about that." He ran his hand along the back of his neck then said, "A minute ago, you said something about things going too fast. What did you mean?"

I put the playing board in the box and took a step toward him, thinking of the huge task he'd taken on—essentially parenting a pre-teen. Most guys in their twenties wouldn't even consider doing it, but Alex had. It was odd in a way. I already thought Alex was attractive, but seeing the way he interacted with Grace and how much he cared for her, just made my heart warm to him even more. Strange that when you get to know someone their inner qualities can become even more attractive than their exterior looks. "You and me...the togetherness of it."

Alex slid the box's lid into place. "The togetherness?"

"You know, holding hands, kissing. Those things."

Alex moved the game to the back of the kitchen counter, then wrapped his arms around me. With his face inches from mine, he said, "Well, she's just going to have to get used to those things. I'm not giving up hand-holding and kissing." He proceeded to demonstrate just how important kissing was.

"Completely agree. Vital thing—kissing," I said a little later. "Very important." I rested my forehead against his. "But you're all Grace has. With your dad in...where is he again? Which embassy?"

"Chile."

"With him in Chile, and your mom..." I trailed off because Alex never said much about his mom.

"In the sunshine somewhere, I'm sure. She left Monte Carlo—I know that—but she hasn't called me since then."

"So, you're it, big brother. Grace needs you. No wonder she is a little…ambivalent toward me. She doesn't want me to take you away as well."

"Hmm…depends on where you want to go, of course. Anywhere with air conditioning sounds good about now."

"From the way the corner of your mouth turned up, I know you're joking, but," I looked over my shoulder to check that the hallway was empty, "Grace might worry. I have no intention of taking you away from her, but she doesn't know that. It will only come with time."

"But things will change. They have to."

"Do they?" I asked. This was as far as we'd drifted into talking about our future. I had a tendency to over-think every aspect of a relationship, but I'd managed to refrain from that bad habit so far with Alex. Mostly. I'd been living in the moment, trying not to look too far down the road—that was when I tended to have my freak-out moments, either clinging so tightly to someone that *they* freaked out, or dropping them when I realized there was a slim chance that the relationship might progress.

I hadn't had the best role models for a loving relationship so with only television and movies as my guide, I was feeling my way in the dark. Usually I "made a hash of it," as Louise would phrase it, but with Alex it had been different. He was easy to be with, and we'd been so busy working that there hadn't been a spare moment to contemplate that big issue: *where was this relationship going?*

Grace's door opened. Alex and I stepped apart like guilty lovers surprised by a chaperone in a Regency novel.

"Alex—" Grace stepped into the hall. "Oh. Hi, Kate. I didn't know you were here."

Her lackluster tone reassured me I'd made the right decision. I needed to bow out of their immediate area for a bit. "I was just leaving." I gave Alex a quick, chaste kiss then waved to Grace. "Have fun at the ruins." I looked at her bored face and added, "If you go, that is."

~

I SUPPOSE most house party guests didn't arrive on foot at Parkview Hall. The blond-haired young man inside the ticket kiosk started guiltily when I leaned in the little window and said hello.

He quickly pocketed his phone and grabbed a clipboard. "You're here for the house party?"

"Yes, Kate Sharp."

A sign posted near the kiosk listed the days and times the estate was open for public tours. A wooden placard had been placed on two hooks at the top of the sign and proclaimed, "Closed for a private event."

He checked my name off his list, then leaned forward to peer out the window. Noting my hastily packed suitcase and the absence of a car, he said, "Would you like for me to call for a ride for you? I'd run you up to the Hall, but I'm not supposed to leave."

"No, it's fine. I like to walk."

"The drive is quite long."

"I know," I said happily and set off along the road that twisted through a grove of oaks. The breeze ruffled the leaves at the tops of the trees, and a bird called sharply as I strode through the dappled sunlight and shade. One of my favorite things about Nether Woodsmoor was how easy it was to walk. Ancient trails crisscrossed the countryside. Exploring them, *rambling* as it was termed here, was always high on my list. The rainy spring with its constant deluges made me appreciate being outdoors even more than I normally would.

As I left the shade of the trees, I paused to admire the view of Parkview Hall with its divided central staircase that curved up to towering double doors. Corinthian columns flanked the imposing doors and supported a portico. I knew from touring the house that two wings stretched out behind the central block of the house, creating a U-shape. From this angle I could only see the east wing and the front of the house. The bright sunlight beat down on the view. The stones caught the light, glowing their mellow golden hue, which contrasted sharply with the bright green of the lawns. In the distance behind the house on the gently rolling hills, sheep grazed. It was so picture-perfect, it could have been a landscape painting, something in the rococo style with its idealized landscapes and perfect tiny people in Georgian dress dotting the landscape.

I trekked along the drive and bypassed the sign for tour parking that took visitors to an area conveniently hidden by a grove of trees. I paused at the sweep of the driveway in front of the stairs. I'd visited Parkview Hall as a tourist and had entered through a side entrance. A few other times, Beatrice had taken me inside to the kitchen through a corridor on the other side of the house near the old stables.

But today I was a guest of the house party. The tour entrance was probably closed, and the kitchen didn't seem like the way I should enter either. I should at least *try* the front door.

I hauled my suitcase up the curving flight of stairs and stepped gratefully into the cool shade of the portico. Before I had time to search for a doorbell, one of the doors that had to be at least fifteen feet high swung open. A small man with wispy hair, wearing a black swallowtail coat over a black waistcoat and dark pants intoned, "Welcome, Miss Sharp."

I resisted the urge to look behind me for a more important personage. He sounded as if he should be announcing a prime minister, at the very least. Instead, I bumped my suitcase over the threshold and entered the lofty black and white tiled entry of Parkview Hall.

I wished Beatrice had given me a quick primer on how to

speak to a butler, but since she hadn't I channeled all those Regency novels I was so fond of and said, "Thank you. You must be Waverly."

He inclined his head. "Lady Stone would like to speak to you. Would you like to retire to your room first?" His voice echoed up to the fresco on the ceiling. How did such a small man have such a carrying voice?

"Yes, I would."

"Very good." Waverly looked over my shoulder. "Thomas will show you to the Rose bedroom."

I turned and jumped. A young man in cream and pale blue livery with a powdered white wig had silently appeared behind me. He took my suitcase from me and began a stately—yet silent —progress across the checkerboard floor. At the foot of the marble staircase he paused and collapsed the suitcase's extendable handle, then he picked it up by the handgrip and resumed his measured pace up the ornate runner patterned in red, blue, green, and yellow. The stairs branched at a landing into a gallery that wrapped around the entire entry hall.

Thomas turned to the right, and I followed him, glancing up as I walked by a stuffed polar bear, claws poised in midair. I looked over the banister to the entry below. Waverly had disappeared, and I wondered how he had known I had arrived. Maybe the teen at the kiosk had called to inform the butler I was on the way, or perhaps there was modern technology at work. I wondered if Parkview was fitted out with cameras to monitor the grounds.

My room was about halfway down the corridor that formed the east wing. I was wondering how I would distinguish exactly which room was mine and was thinking that I'd have to remember my door was to the right of a huge glass display cabinet filled with framed collections of butterflies, crystals, and seashells, but then I noticed a square metal frame about the size of a business card near the door Thomas had just entered. My name, written in calligraphy, was on a small white card inside the frame. I'd read about the country house parties that had been given when bed hopping was practically a sport among a certain set of the aristocracy. How handy to have names noted outside doors. I'm sure that prevented rather embarrassing mistakes, and, on the practical side, it would be helpful to the servants.

I followed Thomas into my room, which was bigger than my whole cottage. "The Rose bedroom, miss," Thomas said.

A thick pale pink and gold carpet covered the floorboards. The same shade of pink was echoed in a pattern of roses on the silk of the canopied bed and on a set of chairs situated on either side of a white-mantled fireplace, which had a relief of delicate swirls and loops decorating it. A dressing table was positioned on one side of the bed, a desk stood near the window, and a dresser topped with a pitcher and bowl stood in one corner near a screen covered in rose silk.

Bowls of pink and white roses were scattered around the room, their scent filling the air. Light streamed in through two sets of floor-to-ceiling glass doors. "A balcony. How lovely." A hook and eye door latch held the doors closed. I flipped the hook out of the metal circle and pushed the door open. The balcony was several feet deep and contained a round iron table and two chairs. At either end of the balcony near the thick stone balusters stood two conical boxwood plants in planters.

Thomas said, "In this wing, only this suite and the room next door, the Mahogany bedroom, have balconies. It is the same across the courtyard, the Versailles and the Oriental bedrooms have balconies."

The balcony overlooked a spacious paved courtyard dotted with more tubs of boxwoods interspersed with benches. At the center of the courtyard, a fountain burbled. The west wing enclosed the far side of the courtyard. The central front block of the house made the south side of the courtyard while another, lower, block of rooms ran along the north, completing the enclosure. It was a lovely view. I'd have to make sure I spent a little time out there during the weekend so I could enjoy it.

As I stepped back into the room, Thomas was putting my suitcase on top of a trunk near the screen, and I wondered if I should tip him. But when I reached for my purse, he gave a small shake of his head while keeping his face otherwise impassive. "Shall I leave the key here?" He set the gold skeleton key with a pink tassel on the writing desk.

"Yes, please."

He bowed and exited, sliding quietly out the door as a young woman with red hair in a braid under a white cap entered and curtsied. She wore a dark cotton dress with a white apron over it. I could just see the tips of her black boots poking out from the hem.

"I'm Ella, miss. I will unpack for you." She was already moving toward my suitcase.

"Um, that's not necessary." The thought of someone else hanging up my clothes or putting my underwear in drawers gave me a distinctly odd feeling. It was beginning to dawn on me that being waited on hand and foot meant a huge loss of privacy. "It's not much. I'll take care of it. Thank you, though."

"Shall I help you change?" She moved to one wall of the room, which had been fitted with cabinets from the floor to ceiling. They looked like a more modern addition to the room than everything else, but I bet that they were still at least fifty years old. She opened one of the doors, revealing a closet area with several full-length dresses hanging from a rod. Shoes, everything from delicate slippers to heavy boots with long laces, filled the lower part of the closet.

I moved across the room and pushed the hangers along the rack. The clothes were all Regency style with high Empire waists. The material ranged from a sturdy patterned muslin to delicate silk. Bonnets lined the shelf above the dresses. "Oh my," I said. *Clothing provided*, that's what Elise had said, but the thought of wearing these exquisite gowns with their fine fabric and ornate trim was a bit intimidating. "Are all the guests changing into period clothing?"

"No, miss, not so far. Most are keeping their modern clothes, at least until tonight at dinner. You have to dress for dinner. Did you bring an evening gown?" Ella glanced doubtfully at my small rolling suitcase.

"No." Well, I would cross that bridge when I came to it. I would have to have help getting into these clothes, that was a given, I thought, running my gaze down the row of tiny buttons at the back of one of the gowns. So privacy and modesty were out the window, at least where your maid was concerned. I squared my shoulders. Since I had been given the part of a lady— with a lady's maid to boot—I better start acting it. "I will change later," I said. "Now, Bea—er, Lady Stone, is expecting me. Can you show me where her office is?"

"Yes, miss." She curtsied. "She'll be in the estate office. If you'll follow me?"

As she turned away, I frowned. "Wait. Aren't you—" I studied her face. Under the drooping flounce of the cap, she did look familiar. "Ella. You're Ella from the pub."

"I don't know what you mean, miss."

"You work for Louise at the White Duck. I'm in there all the time."

She shot a quick guilty look at the open door, then lowered her voice. "We're not supposed to break character."

I matched her soft tone. "Oh, I see."

"I'm off from the pub this weekend, and the immersive experience is wonderful practice."

"Practice?"

"For acting. I have my application in for a drama school in London."

"How exciting. I didn't know."

Her face lit up as she grinned from ear to ear. "Only Louise knows. I haven't told anyone else."

"Well, in that case, I'll try to stay in character as well. How should I address you?"

"A lady calls her maid by her last name. Mine is Tewkesbury," she said half apologetically, but a smile lurked at the corners of her mouth.

"Very well," I said, thinking of Lady Catherine de Bourgh in *Pride and Prejudice*, who had referred to her maid as Dawson. If Lady Catherine's maid had the misfortune to be named Tewkesbury I'm sure Lady Catherine would have changed it to "Smith" immediately.

"Lead on, Tewkesbury," I said. I shoved the key, tassel and all, into my pocket.

She curtsied and took me unerringly along the corridors lined with paintings, tapestries, and statues, then down a set of stairs and into the other wing of the house. It seemed these rooms had been made into the headquarters of the business side of Parkview. We passed a sturdy metal door, which looked out of place, compared to the elaborate wainscoting and the other doors along the hallway, which were made of rich wood and deeply paneled. I caught a peek inside the narrow glass window set into the metal door. Banks of computer monitors, each displaying a different image filled the wall. A man in a navy blazer sat in front of the monitors, a huge control panel and computer situated in front of him. Ella noticed my interest. "That's the monitoring room." She lowered her voice. "Eyes are always on you here."

"Are they?" I guess that answered my question about how the staff had known I'd arrived.

Ella kept her voice low. "You can't blame them. The house is full of valuables—paintings, silver, old books, and artifacts brought back from other countries. They have to keep watch, I suppose. It does give me the shivers when I think about it...that someone could watch me on the monitors, tracing every step I take throughout the house."

"It's that extensive?" I asked, surprised.

"Oh yes. One maid was let go when she tried to steal a little jade figurine from a cabinet in the west hallway. She figured no one would see her, but they knew," Ella said, throwing a glance back at the metal door. "They stopped her on the way down the stairs."

We approached the end of the hallway, and Ella must have suddenly remembered that she wasn't in character. She straightened her shoulders and made her face properly blank as she guided me into a suite of rooms with several desks in an outer office, which were empty at the moment. The room was less grand than the other parts of the house, but despite being filled with desks, swivel chairs, and computer monitors, the tall windows framed with heavy drapes and the chandelier overhead made the room swankier than any office I'd ever worked in.

"Impressive. Not one wrong turn."

"Thank you. There was a test," she said in an undertone then looked stricken, I suppose because she'd broken character again.

I heard Beatrice's voice through a door that opened off the main room. Ella—I couldn't think of her as Tewkesbury—walked ahead of me to the open door. "Miss Kate, your ladyship." A sudden chorus of high-pitched barks followed Ella's announcement, and two little white fur balls made a beeline for me.

I had met Beatrice's dogs before. Despite their rather territorial reaction, they were harmless. I scratched their ears and let them lick my hand with their scratchy tongues then Beatrice called them back to their cushion behind her desk where they settled down, heads on their paws, bright eyes on Beatrice.

Ella had backed out of the doorway and let me enter, but I realized she was hovering uncertainly in the outer office.

I remembered my role of Regency lady. I discreetly wiped the dog slobber off the back of my hands onto the legs of my jeans as I said, "That will be all, —er, Tewkesbury."

She bobbed again, and I thought that besides all the actual work of being a maid, her legs must be exhausted, just from the curtsying alone.

"Kate, so glad you're here." Behind her expansive desk, which was covered in reams of paper, Beatrice removed a set of glasses and rubbed the bridge of her nose with one hand as she waved me into her office with the other. "Come in. Close the door, if you don't mind."

Like everything else in Parkview Hall, the door was oversized, at least eight feet tall. I gripped the worn gold handle and pulled the ornately paneled door closed then dropped into the seat of a modern club chair across from Beatrice.

"How is your room? Everything acceptable?"

"It's gorgeous. I love it. I'm not sure about the Regency aspect, though. I didn't brush up on my protocol."

"You'll be fine. That's why we don't usually stand on ceremony here. Standing on ceremony is quite tiring. We only do it now because the house party guests expect it. Our first Regency house party weekend was two weeks ago. Everyone loves the clothes and the idea of returning to an earlier time, but after a day or so, the romance of it wears off."

"Still, I'll probably call someone by the wrong name—or won't even remember their name." In polite society it would have been much harder to hide a bad memory for names than in our modern world where "girl" and "dude" were acceptable forms of address.

"You'll get a welcome packet with all the guest names and a short bio on each one, an effort on our part to make the house party seem more like a real party. Some of the guests would have known each other at these types of events. To replicate that atmosphere, we mailed packets with guest bios and information about Parkview last week to all our attendees. We'll have place cards tonight at dinner, too. That will help," Beatrice said then smiled suddenly. "And you can also blame it on being an American."

"Yes, that covers a multitude of sins, especially etiquette sins." I relaxed back in the chair. Despite being the lady of the manor, Beatrice was incredibly easy to talk to. She didn't put on airs and was as unpretentious as you could get. "Still, I'll probably use the wrong fork at dinner."

"You can use whatever fork you want, of course. The secret is to do it with panache. Panache covers a multitude of sins as well."

"Hmm. Must work on my panache quotient, then."

Beatrice tapped her glasses against a wobbly pile of papers, her face turning serious. "I'm so glad you're here. I asked you for an entirely selfish reason." She paused as if reluctant to go on then said, "I hope you can help me with...well, I suppose if this were a few years ago, I'd call them poison pen letters, but they're not letters. It is the modern equivalent, though, showing up every three days." She turned a key in a lock on a desk drawer and removed a file then handed it across to me. "I printed those out before Holly deleted them."

I looked through the first pages, recognizing the familiar layouts of social media sites. The printed pages were screen shots of Parkview Hall's Facebook, Twitter, and Instagram feeds. I knew Parkview Hall had a website. I'd done some photography work for them, but I wasn't aware that the estate also had these accounts, but it made sense business-wise. It paid to have an online presence, no matter what business you were in. The stately home touring business was like any other enterprise. People would search for information about estate tours online, and Parkview Hall could promote its events through social media.

I skimmed down the first page and stopped, surprised to see a comment on Parkview Hall's Facebook page that read, "These people are greedy and evil. Horrible."

I flicked through the next pages, which contained more of the same caustic tone repeated in slightly different forms. *Grasping and mercenary. Don't waste your time.*

"So angry," I said. "Do you know why? There aren't any details."

Beatrice put her glasses down, and a pile of papers slithered toward the floor. She shoved them back. "At first, I thought it was a coincidence. You know, a few people had bad experiences and vented. Some of the tourists do become quite unreasonable over the smallest things. One woman threw a fit because we don't let anyone enter the library to take photographs. She demanded a refund on her entrance fee."

"Wow."

Beatrice shrugged a shoulder. "It happens. I've always known that you can't please everyone, but working with the public day in and day out makes that fact crystal clear. I know that a small portion of people who tour Parkview Hall go away disgruntled. But this is more than that. Keep reading."

I ran through more posts with the same general venomous tone, but the two printouts at the bottom of the stack were different. One had a photo of Sir Harold seated in a wingback chair. He held a crystal tumbler of what looked to be brandy or whiskey loosely balanced on the arm of the chair while in the foreground of the photo, the sharp edges of a crystal decanter rested on the table in front of him. His head was tilted back, and the photograph had caught him at a moment when his eyes were half closed and his mouth was partially open, giving him a drunken look. The text under the photo read, "Sir Harold overindulges, his favorite past time—other than raising the rents."

The last printout showed another image of Sir Harold. This time, he was on the drive in front of Parkview Hall and appeared to be embracing a young woman with red hair. The text claimed, "Sir Harold can't contain himself even in public. He would make a laughable Lothario except that the focus of his attentions are the lowest female staff."

I looked up from the pages. "But this makes no sense. Sir Harold?" No matter how I stretched my imagination, I could not picture Sir Harold as either a drunk or as someone who would fool around with the staff. Granted, I hadn't been around Sir Harold as much as I had been around Beatrice, but he had always been extremely courteous with me. He had the manners and old-world gallantry that weren't usually in evidence today. Well, when he came out of his reverie, that is.

Sir Harold always seemed to be immersed in some project. The last time I'd talked with him, when we met outside the church after services on Sunday, we'd had a nice chat about his efforts to improve the output of honey from Parkview Hall's beehives. Most of the time he had the glassy, faraway look on his face as if his thoughts were physically surrounding him, partially blocking out what was going on around him. The idea of him even noticing the female staff in that way...well, it went completely against every indication I had about his personality and character.

Beatrice nodded. "Yes, a load of claptrap, all of it. Harold does well to notice *me* a few times a day." She paused to smile. "Which I know is not saying much. I'm no beauty, but you know what Harold is like. He doesn't notice *anyone*—male or female. The thought that he's stalking the young females in our employ is... well, it would be laughable if it weren't such a serious allegation."

She pointed to the paper in my hand. "That last photo was taken a week ago. I was two steps behind him, speaking to Mrs. King, our housekeeper, when Harold stumbled. Ella happened to be right there, thank goodness, and managed to catch his arm before he fell. Unfortunately, photos can be cropped to make it look like they were alone. And they can be manipulated, like the one of him in the chair. No one looks healthy and alert in every photo. Apparently, if you have your film set at the right speed you can catch anyone looking terrible."

"Yes, that is true." I was by no means a photography expert, but I'd learned enough that I knew the person taking the photos could either make a location look fabulous or awful, simply with a few changes of settings. I'd once photographed a sitting room of a cozy little house as a potential location for an interview scene on a television crime drama. The lens made the room look huge, but my boss, who was training me, pointed out that despite how good the room looked in the photos, the producer and director would be furious if they got there and couldn't get the cast and their equipment into the small room.

I was sure the same principle applied to photographing people. Even though I didn't focus on taking pictures of people, I usually caught a few bystanders or fellow crew members in my shots, and often just the tilt of their head or angle of their body made the photos unflattering.

"I'm sorry you've had to deal with this." I handed the file back, at a loss for what else to say. My thoughts were churning, not sure what else I could say to help with Beatrice's "spot of bother."

She carefully replaced the file in the drawer and locked it. "But why am I showing them to you?" She folded her hands together and leaned forward. "I think you can help me figure out who is doing this."

"Me?" I said weakly. I was afraid I knew where this discussion was going. "Just because the...what did you call them...the poisoned pen posts had photographs, doesn't mean I'm the person you need. My expertise is not in photography, not really. If you want me to find a room for a commercial shoot or a room that can double as a Regency ballroom, then I'm your girl, but this is way out of my league."

"No, that's not why I thought of you. Although, you did take some lovely photos of Parkview for the website. No, I need you for three reasons: you're clever, you're observant, and—most important—you are an outsider."

I shook my head. "Shouldn't you contact Constable Albertson? Someone official, anyway. Those statements are libelous. The police could try and track down the source of the posts. They could get that information. I can't do that."

Beatrice waved her hand. "Impossible. I have a friend whose son is a whiz at this computer stuff. He moved to California a few years ago to work for some important computer company...can't remember the name. But that doesn't matter. I had him look into it, remotely of course. Gave him access to our end of the social media accounts. He said the person camouflaged themselves."

She frowned. "I'm not at all sure he didn't engage in some rather iffy actions to produce that knowledge, but he assured me it would be fine. I wouldn't have asked if I'd realized it might not all be on the right side of the law, but what's done is done, and we might as well use the information. He said the person protected their computer through something he called redirects, I believe. The long and short of it was that the trail is cold and even if the police had a warrant they couldn't discover who created those posts. The trail simply bounces around the globe, it seems." Beatrice shrugged then her face changed, taking on a conspiratorial look. "But I was able to narrow it down from the whole world to the employees of Parkview Hall."

"How did you do that?" I asked, intrigued.

"The posts that are only words," she shrugged again, "impossible to discern much from them. They came from various dummy accounts, which were obviously set up to enable the anonymous person to post those horrible things. The accounts were generic and had hardly any information on them. When the first posts popped up, I discounted them, as I said. In fact, I didn't even think to check the accounts that the posts came from. By the time I caught on, some of the accounts had already been deleted or suspended. Once I realized it wasn't just upset tourists,

I researched the accounts, gathering all the information I could. Unfortunately, deleting the posts from our feeds on our end was all we could do. I contacted the social media sites, but they weren't helpful. They banned the accounts, but two days later, another scurrilous post would appear under another account name. A hopeless situation, really, except for the photos. As much as I didn't want to look at them, I studied them and discovered something. Both photos were taken during a time when Parkview was closed to visitors, so that means the photographer has to be someone on staff."

She grimaced as if she'd eaten something that tasted bad. "As much as it pains me to think it, we're not the happy family I thought we were. The photo outdoors was taken last week during one of the days we were closed to visitors. The one with Harold in the chair with a drink was taken later that same day. It's ironic. Harold doesn't drink that much, but because I had a drink, he joined me. So you see, it has to be someone who was here when the house wasn't open to visitors, which naturally means a staff member."

"Have you considered the possibility that the images are from two different people?"

"No," Beatrice said quickly. "I checked. They were posted from the same account, Chris Robert's account, by the way."

"Hmm...not very helpful, but at least it wasn't Smith."

Beatrice let out a snort. "No, that would be too obviously fake, wouldn't it?"

My smile faded as I said, "So you want me to...spy on your employees? Try to catch someone in the act of taking more photographs?"

"No, I simply want you to keep your eyes and ears open. Observe the staff. You have the opportunity to be here uninterrupted for the whole weekend. You were able to ferret out several tiny details that made all the difference in those other cases. See if you notice anything here at Parkview."

"On the surface that doesn't sound that hard, but what if I don't see anything? I'd hate to let you down."

"Well, then I suppose you'll have had a nice weekend—I hope you enjoy it—and I'll have to resort to calling in a private detective." She sighed. "We can't let these rumors go unchecked. Besides the damage it does on the publicity front, it also seems to be escalating."

She had a point. The first posts only insinuated that the inhabitants of Parkview were greedy, but the last attacks had been more specific—focused solely at Sir Harold and accusing him of being an alcoholic and a womanizer, accusations that you wouldn't want directed at you personally, but there was another aspect to the situation. As the head of the Stone family, Sir Harold also headed the business organization that was Parkview Hall. Although, it seemed from what I'd seen that Sir Harold pursued his own interests while Beatrice handled the day-to-day running of Parkview. But he was still the top figure at Parkview, and I could see why Beatrice would want to put a stop to the posts.

"Does anyone else here at Parkview know what you've found out?"

"Only Harold." She looked at the drifts of paper covering her desk. "Quite shook him up. There's not much that will draw him out of his own interior world, but this certainly has. Of course, Holly deals with our social media, so she knows about the posts. She's the one who first pointed them out to me, but she doesn't know that I've narrowed it—"

A quick tap sounded on the door, then it swung open. A slender young woman stepped across the threshold, but stopped short when she saw me. "Oh, excuse me." She wore the uniform of Parkview Hall employees, a navy blazer and matching skirt, the same uniform that the guides wore as they escorted tourists through the building, but the business attire didn't sit on her easily. The formal lines of it were at odds with the casual cut of her white-blond hair, which was short in the back, but a long swath of bangs fell forward over one side of her face. She quickly swept her bangs to the side and tucked them behind an ear, revealing a heart-shaped face with dark arched brows, blue eyes, and a sprinkling of freckles. She didn't have on much makeup, only pink lipstick and a bit of mascara. "I heard your voice, but I thought you were on the phone," she said to Beatrice.

"It's fine," Beatrice said. "Come in, Holly. This is Kate Sharp, one of our guests for the weekend."

Holly tucked a computer tablet into the crook of her arm and stepped into the room. "Nice to meet you. Holly Riley."

"Holly is our publicity director," Beatrice said. "She's a genius at all this new media, thank goodness, which means I don't have to deal with it."

I said hello to Holly and shook her hand, thinking that Beatrice was being modest. She was obviously up to speed enough on social media to delete the posts and research the accounts behind them.

"I'm so glad I ran into you." Holly handed me a folder that had been tucked under her tablet. "Your introductory packet. Maps of the house, schedules of when the kitchen is open for room service, and phone numbers for all our services. If you'd like to ride or book a spa appointment, all the contact information is in there as well as the personal profiles the guests provided for this weekend. Oh, and a schedule of activities, of course. Everything is optional, but most people have participated in at least a few of the activities. The garden and house tours are always the most popular. I'm sorry I didn't have time to update the packet with your information," Holly said.

"Don't worry about it. Nothing much interesting about me."

"That's not what I've heard," Holly said with a grin that could only be described as impish. "Word among the staff is that you are quite the investigator."

I didn't look toward Beatrice, but out of the corner of my eye I saw her stiffen.

"You know what they say about rumors, that there's hardly ever any truth in them. No, I'm looking forward to relaxing. I'm a big Jane Austen fan and want to discover what a Regency house party was like."

"Wonderful," Holly said then turned to Beatrice. "The Funderburgs are on their way up from the gate. I thought you'd want to meet them."

"Yes, of course." Beatrice stood and smoothed her dress, which I noticed for the first time since we'd begun talking. Beatrice usually didn't have much interest in fashion. Mostly I'd seen her in her boxy raincoat, which had gotten a lot of use this spring. On Sundays, I'd seen her at the village church in loose cardigans and wide skirts that she wore with espadrille sandals. Today she looked more fashionable than I'd ever seen her. She wore a short-sleeved sheath dress in a nubby pale blue fabric. It was decorated with a double row of gold buttons, that gave it a slightly military air. The severe cut suited her square body type. As she stepped out from the desk, she said, "Would you like to walk with us? We can take you back to the entry hall."

"Yes, that would be good. I won't get lost," I said as I followed Beatrice through the outer office and into the hall. I fell into step beside her, her black pumps striking the tile floor, each step ringing out like a gunshot. With her monochromatic dress and dark pumps she reminded me a bit of the queen.

"I sent Thomas to bring Sir Harold," Holly said.

"Good."

CHAPTER 3

$\mathcal{W}$E ARRIVED IN THE ENTRY just as Waverly appeared and crossed the hall toward the enormous double doors. Sir Harold drifted down the grand staircase, his bald head bent over a book held in his liver-spotted hands. Beatrice aligned herself with the door, and Holly faded backward until she was almost inside the huge fireplace that filled one wall. If she'd ducked her head an inch or so she would have been able to step inside it easily.

"Showtime, Waverly," Beatrice murmured under her breath.

"Indeed," Waverly said in his dignified tones.

Sir Harold walked unerringly to Beatrice's side, closed the book, which I saw was a field guide to butterflies, then slipped it into his pocket. Every time I'd seen him, he'd been wearing a shirt, tie, and dress pants. Today he'd added a suit jacket. "Hello, my dear," he said to Beatrice as he blinked and glanced around the entry as if he'd just stepped off an elevator onto an unfamiliar floor and didn't quite know which way to turn.

Beatrice smoothed his lapel. "Guests, dear. For the house party."

"Right. Of course. House party." Sir Harold caught sight of me as I slipped through the hall on my way to the grand staircase. "Hello, Kate," he said. "I understand you are staying for the weekend as well."

"Yes. I'm looking forward to it."

"Excellent. Delighted to have you."

"Thank you," I said, struck again by Sir Harold's vague, but courtly manners. He might spend most of his time in his own mental world, but he was courteous and kind. In fact, the first time I'd met him, he'd made me tea when I was shaken up because there had been an accident. Of course, no one was perfect, but I couldn't imagine Sir Harold doing any of the things described in the poisoned pen posts.

Just thinking about the accusations as I looked over Sir Harold's vague, yet welcoming face next to Beatrice's strained face, irritated me. Who would do such a thing to such nice people?

They were giving it their all to keep Parkview Hall open, partly because of the familial connection to the place, but also because it was the largest employer in the village. Who would want to trash their reputation? And who would post nasty things about such a benign, gentle person?

I turned to climb the grand staircase, determined to keep my eyes open. I wasn't sure I'd be much help to them, but I could try. Beatrice called out, "Kate, why don't you stay and meet our guests?"

"Yes, I suppose I should." I came back down the stairs, but didn't move off to the side of the entry like Holly did. She was busily tapping away on her phone in the shadows.

The entry hall became lighter as Waverly heaved open one of the doors and intoned, "Mr. and Mrs. Jay Funderburg."

Beatrice stepped forward. "Welcome to Parkview," she said to an Indian woman with beautiful brown skin and black hair. Its glossy waves brushed a scarf of turquoise, pink, and cream that rested on her shoulders. She wore a cream-colored linen pantsuit and matching three-inch heels. I could tell from the cut of the suit that it was expensive. Her look—polished and exclusive—reminded me of some of the Hollywood executives I'd crossed paths with occasionally in my early location scouting days when my boss brought me along to meetings as I learned the ropes. But when Beatrice introduced us, Mrs. Funderburg wasn't distracted or disinterested. Her gaze was expressive and warm as she shook my hand.

"Please, call me Jo," she said as she gripped my hand in a handshake so firm I had to hide a wince.

"Oh, you're American," I said. "It's so nice to hear a familiar accent."

"Yes, everyone expects me to have a British accent here," she said with a smile, "but I'm American, born and bred. I grew up in Florida. Where are you from?"

"California."

"Well, excellent," Sir Harold murmured, and I think we were both waiting for him to ask if we might have some common acquaintances, but thankfully he didn't fall into that cliché.

"And Mr. Funderburg," Beatrice added, neatly moving Jo's husband from Sir Harold to me.

"Yes, of course," I said quickly, shifting to include him in the conversation. Jo was such a presence with her exotic beauty and friendly smile that she eclipsed her husband. I'd completely forgotten he was in the room, but he was there, hovering a little behind Jo.

A slightly paunchy middle-aged man with curly brown hair, he was about two inches shorter than his wife, and his clothes were as casual as Jo's were dressy. But he didn't look the least bit intimidated or worried that he was underdressed in his white polo shirt, khaki cargo shorts, and leather sandals. He hovered slightly behind Jo, looking content to let her do all the talking. "Jay," he said, shoving a large smartphone into his pocket and extending his hand.

I returned his greeting, and Beatrice said, "First names are fine for now, but tonight we'll use formal address at dinner. We must be Regency appropriate for at least one night." She looked toward Waverly. "Tea?"

"Being served on the terrace," he said, his face expressionless.

"Very good." Beatrice turned back to the Funderburgs. "Perhaps you'd like to freshen up then join us for tea?"

"Sounds wonderful," Jo said.

"Thomas will show you to your room," Beatrice said as Thomas floated out of one of the deep corners of the room, already toting two large suitcases. I noticed the couple exchange a quick smile before following Thomas up the staircase. It was one of those quiet glances that I'd sometimes seen married couples exchange, full of meaning and only for each other. Holly quickly closed the distance to Beatrice and drew her into a discussion over the tablet as they went back toward the estate office. Sir Harold nodded and drifted toward the library.

I turned, intending to go to the terrace, but I faltered after only a few steps. The house was huge, and the only times I'd walked through it before had been when areas were roped off and guides directed you along a path that wound through the rooms.

A chorus of voices in a soprano pitch echoed up to the vaulted ceiling as three young women came down the grand staircase. A curvy woman with black corkscrew curls cut in a long bob and a porcelain complexion was at the center of the group. She wore distressed skinny jeans with a white T-shirt with the word "Bride" stitched in curly font. She swiped her finger across her phone, then held it out to her two companions. "Did you see this one? Isn't it just too, too gorgeous?"

A lanky woman on her right, her thin blond hair caught back in a ponytail, which was additionally secured with a thin headband, smiled perfunctorily. "Cute." She wore black running shorts, a hot pink sleeveless workout top in a dry weave fabric, and expensive running shoes. Her face was free of makeup, and her hair was damp around the hairline.

The petite woman on the other side of the bride wore black jeans and a white top with a cowl neckline. Her dark brown hair feathered around her face. She had a small mouth and large dark eyes. She looked at the phone longer, then said, "Umm, very sparkly, but don't you think it might be a bit much? For a head-piece, I mean. You want everyone looking at your face, not your tiara, right?"

"See, that's why I brought you, Amanda. You're so sensible." The woman in the bride shirt pounded down the last few steps, her generous bosom bouncing. She spotted me. "Oh, another new person. Hello, I'm Beth Coleson. At least for now, I am. In a year, I'll be Mrs. Hugo Stanhope-Smithy." Her tone indicated that I should recognize the name of her fiancée. "These are my bridesmaids. We're planning the wedding this weekend. I thought it best to get away so we could give it our complete concentration."

"How...nice," I said and introduced myself.

Beth grinned happily at me then pointed to her lanky blond friend, "This is Torrie Peters. She has no interest in all this wedding stuff at all, but she's been my best friend since we were three so she's my chief bridesmaid."

Torrie trotted down the last steps and shook my hand. "I'm only here to make sure there are no bows or ruffles," she said flatly. "I don't do well in ruffles."

It didn't sound like Torrie had much interest in fashion, but it did seem she had good instincts when it came to her body type. Fussy, frilly styles wouldn't go with her rather boyish build.

"And this is Amanda Atherton," Beth said, turning to her brunette friend, who glided down the last few steps and extended her hand. "Amanda is a chef."

"Sous-chef," Amanda said quickly.

Beth rolled her eyes and waved off the distinction. "She makes sublime desserts. She's making my cake and helping with...well, everything else. She's so organized and efficient."

"So are you interested in the Regency weekend?" I asked.

"Sure. It's a nice bonus. What we really needed was the peace and quiet of this weekend to plan. Although, it will be so much fun to dress up. I absolutely adore dressing up." Beth squeezed her shoulders together and wrinkled her nose.

I glanced around the group and noticed Torrie looked less than enthusiastic. Amanda had a half smile on her face and was shaking her head slightly. Her expression might have been captioned, "resigned exasperation," which made me wonder if she was more an unpaid wedding planner than a friend. Beth's face went serious. "Of course the Regency stuff is fun and all, but we can't forget the real reason we're here—my wedding."

I suspected that no one in Beth's immediate vicinity would be allowed to forget it.

"Why are you here? Are you with anyone else?" Beth asked, her gaze roving around the corners of the entry.

"No, I'm on my own. I'm doing research." I left it at that. I'd met people like Beth before and knew that despite her declaration of being solely interested in planning her wedding, if I mentioned the words *television documentary production*, she'd be after me like a magpie after a shiny trinket. "Are you on your way to tea? I'm looking for the terrace and don't know how to get there."

"Come with us." Beth linked her arm through mine. "Amanda knows the way." She nodded for Amanda to go first.

By the time we arrived on the terrace, I'd seen Beth's ring, a diamond so large that I wondered if it would give her carpel tunnel syndrome from the sheer weight of lugging it around. I also learned that Beth had met Amanda at school and various other tidbits about the upcoming wedding, including the date and the potential color schemes and themes, which were still under consideration.

Several café tables and chairs were scattered about the flag-stone terrace, which I recognized as being connected to the larger terrace at the back of the house next to the gift shop where the tours of the house ended. Thirsty tourists often stopped at the tea shop located near that larger terrace before touring Parkview's grounds. This terrace was more intimate and gave a view of a long stretch of parkland with a fountain. Antique tele-scopes were mounted on each end of the terrace.

A few groups of people were already seated, and somehow Beatrice had beat us here. She expertly disengaged me from Beth's group with the excuse that I hadn't met everyone yet. She guided me to a table with a couple who didn't seem to go together at first glance. A woman in her mid-thirties wore a Regency dress of what I supposed was sprigged muslin—it was lightweight and patterned with tiny pink flowers—with cap sleeves and a pink sash. The man at her side looked to be near her age, but he was dressed in modern clothes, dark slacks and a faded blue collared polo shirt that strained over his biceps.

The woman looked up at me from under the brim of her straw bonnet, which covered all of her hair except a few red bangs that brushed her forehead. Beatrice introduced her as Audrey Page. The skin around her eyes crinkled as she smiled. "I couldn't wait to wear period clothes," she said without a hint of self-consciousness. "When I found out about the house party, I was so excited. An opportunity to wear my Regency clothes, and at a true stately home!"

"So the clothes are yours?" I asked.

"Oh, yes. I love Jane Austen and the Regency. I've been making historic clothing for years for other people—sort of a sideline to my real work. I'm in graphic design—freelance, you know, but for years I've wanted to get involved in reenactments, but our girls were too small. Now that they're older, I've decided to join a local chapter, but you must have the correct clothes, so

SARA ROSETT

I've made four dresses for myself. I'm so excited to get to wear them this weekend."

"Your dress is beautiful."

"Thank you." She shot a glance at the burly man beside her. "Now, I just have to get Simon into his coat and breeches tonight. I think he'll love it once he wears it."

He looked up from a notepad. "You've talked me into it this once, but no more." He had a large nose and a gap between his front teeth. He had a rougher vibe than his wife that made me think he might have been a boxer. He bent his shaved head over the paper, and Audrey winked at Beatrice and me. "We'll see."

Simon harrumphed, but didn't contradict her.

Audrey said, "I only managed to convince Simon to come because he's interested in preparedness. He's already had a long chat with the housekeeper about canned food storage."

Simon nodded. "Excellent example of sustainability in the pre-war years."

"We try to carry on the traditions where we're able," Beatrice said then moved me on to the next table, which had a solitary occupant. "Kate, this is Michael Jaffery."

The young man, probably in his early twenties, put his finger in a book with a butterfly on the cover. He was the complete opposite of Simon Page. Thin and rather gawky, his rumpled suit jacket hung on his bony shoulders. He shook my hand and mumbled it was nice to meet me, but kept his head ducked and angular shoulders hunched as if he didn't want to talk. His thin blond hair fell forward against the rims of his circular glasses.

"Mr. Jaffery is writing a book on lepidoptery," Beatrice said.

"Butterflies?" I asked, nodding to the book.

"Yes," he answered me, but I noticed that his gaze was drawn to Amanda as she crossed the terrace.

"He's here to consult the Parkview collection," Beatrice said. "The second baronet was an extensive collector, a study that Sir Harold has also taken up."

Amanda sat down at a table with Beth and Torrie, her back toward us. Michael drew his attention back to us. "It's one of the best collections in Britain," Michael said, reverence in his voice.

"We're glad you could stay for the house party," Beatrice said as Sir Harold ambled over from another group and sat down with Michael, who managed to sit a little straighter.

"Hello, Sir Harold," Michael said. "Frightfully nice of you to invite me to stay."

"Delighted you are here. Now, tell me about your book. I understand you're especially interested in our blues."

I assumed Sir Harold was referring to butterflies, not music, and Beatrice confirmed it with a tilt of her head, indicating we could move on. "They will be at it for hours."

She steered me to the final couple at another table. I did a double take, which I hoped wasn't as noticeable as I feared. If I'd had a chance to read over the packet with the guest bios I wouldn't have been surprised, but I didn't expect to meet two celebrities at the house party.

Beatrice announced, "Mr. and Mrs. Toby Clay," but she didn't have to. This was one couple who I wouldn't have to struggle to remember their names. Toby Clay and his trophy wife Monique were household names, but for completely different reasons.

Toby was a millionaire entrepreneur who dabbled in all sorts of things now, but he'd gotten his start in online gambling, purchasing the domain name Longshot and revamping the site right before online gambling surged in popularity. I don't normally keep up with British movers-and-shakers, but a year or so ago, he'd married Monique Gillbank, who frequently appeared in the tabloid press. It didn't matter how uninterested you were in celebrity news, the couple, which the media dubbed "Tonique," a combination of their two first names, was everywhere—on the covers of the tabloids at the checkout in the grocery, at the news-stand, and on the television news as their relationship became the leading human interest story of last summer.

I supposed the reason for all the hype was that they were an unlikely couple. A relationship between a rich, freshly divorced businessman from his wife of nearly a decade and a young socialite who seemed to move from one train-wreck moment to another was catnip to the celebrity press. Monique was one of those troubled famous people who show up in the news at frequent intervals, the media documenting her every failure and misstep. The fact that she seemed to court the attention, even revel in it, only drew the media to her more.

The family business, Gillbank Pharmaceuticals, was a household name in the States as well as in the U.K. She was the only daughter of the family, and had made a career out of dressing outrageously and getting caught while driving under the influence. The fact that her family was in the drug business had made for some incredibly tacky headlines after her arrest. She'd managed to parley her fifteen minutes of fame into several years of coverage. With her platinum blond hair styled in retro curves, blood-red lips, and white halter-top sundress, she looked as if she were a Marilyn Monroe impersonator.

Toby put down his tea cup and stood as Beatrice introduced me, his gaze running lazily over my figure. He was good-looking with mesmerizing blue eyes in a tan face and had a carelessly charismatic, I-live-the-good-life aura. "Charmed," he said, holding my hand a bit too long. Coming from anyone else, that line would have seemed trite, but he carried it off.

Beatrice introduced me to Monique, who stayed in her chair and only tilted her head an inch, the huge dark ovals of her sunglasses hiding her eyes. Her ruby lips twitched to one side as Toby motioned to a third chair. "Won't you join us?"

I slipped into the chair. Beatrice nodded for a footman to serve me tea, which he did, but only before quietly asking if I would like the welcome packet I'd been carrying around sent to my room. I handed it off, and he traded it for my tea.

"If I could have your attention for a moment." Beatrice had

moved to the center of the terrace. "Sir Harold and I would like to welcome you to Parkview. We hope you enjoy the house party. If you need anything, anything at all, let one of the staff know, and they will take care of you."

I glanced around, remembering that Beatrice had asked me to focus on the staff. I'd been so wrapped up in meeting the other guests and concentrating on names that I hadn't even noticed the staff, but as I looked now, I saw that several of the staff stood around the edge of the terrace, wearing historical uniforms of footmen and maids. Holly hovered inside the doors that opened into a sitting room, her navy blazer blending in with the shadows. If it weren't for her bright whitish blond hair, I would have missed her. Her attention was focused on the computer tablet. Everyone seemed to be doing exactly what they should be—attending to the guests, removing empty cups, or offering plates of cakes and sandwiches.

"To make your experience as immersive as possible, we have one request. Please silence your cell phones and refrain from using them in the common areas. We ask that you be considerate of your fellow guests and abide by this rule. I realize not everyone here is interested in historical accuracy." Beatrice's gaze skimmed over Monique and Toby. "But some guests do want to experience a true Regency house party and that will only be possible if everyone cooperates."

Monique let out a little huff, but changed a setting on her phone, which she had placed on the table beside her teacup. As a couple of the other guests removed phones from purses or pockets and followed Beatrice's request, an orange and black butterfly flittered along a low hedge that surrounded the terrace then drifted toward Audrey's straw bonnet. She patted Simon's arm to get his attention. He was absorbed in watching the other guests, and it took a firmer poke for Audrey to draw his attention, but by then the butterfly had moved on. It dipped near Monique's plate, which contained one sandwich splayed open.

She'd apparently eaten the slice of cucumber and left the bread. The butterfly flitted lower, and Monique whipped her hands back and forth, shooing it away, her long, red fingernails blurring with her almost frantic movements.

Toby didn't move a finger to pull out a cell phone. I wondered if it was because he thought he was above the rules, or if he didn't have a cell phone on him. He struck me as the type of person who would hand off as much as possible to an assistant.

"Thank you," Beatrice said. "Now, on to the more enjoyable things. We dine at seven-thirty tonight, but will meet in the large drawing room at seven for drinks. I look forward to seeing you all in your Regency finest," Beatrice concluded and went to join the Funderburgs. She would introduce them to everyone once they'd had their tea. I never realized what hard work it was to be a hostess.

"Not me," Monique muttered. The screen on her phone flashed with a new message. She tossed her sunglasses on the table and grabbed the phone. Toby sent her a cold glance then explained to me. "My wife doesn't wear anything that isn't couture."

"Well, it would seem that handmade Regency gowns would be about as couture as you could get," I said. "Everything looked to be one of a kind. At least the ones in my room were each unique."

Monique had been tapping out a text, but she paused long enough to give me a pitying stare as she arched one golden eyebrow. She had gorgeous topaz eyes thickly fringed with dark lashes. Now that the glasses were off, I could see that the pictures in the tabloids hadn't done her justice. The combination of high cheekbones, flawless skin, and sculpted lips combined with her unusual golden brown eyes made her a beautiful woman. "I brought my own gowns for dinner." She went back to texting.

Okay, so more beautiful on the outside than the inside.

A chair behind me scraped across the flagstones as Sir Harold rose. "Let me get the monograph to show you." Michael half rose to follow him, but Sir Harold waved him back to his chair. "No, wait here. It is just in the sitting room. Won't be a moment. I was reading it yesterday. It has some interesting information on the Dwarf Blue from South Africa." Sir Harold moved across the terrace to the sitting room.

I returned my attention to my table mates. Toby was frowning at Monique. "Not everyone finds fashion so consuming." Unlike her completely smooth face, his face was rough and the skin wrinkled into deep furrows around his eyes as he smiled an apology at me. "Do you dress for dinner tonight in Regency clothes?"

"Yes. I'll give it an attempt."

I thought I heard a snort from Monique's vicinity, but when I looked her way, she was absorbed in her Twitter feed.

The butterfly reappeared, drawn to our table again, but this time it floated close to Toby and dropped down to the flagstones near his foot.

"I wonder if Michael could tell us what kind it is?" I asked, looking toward Michael, but he was writing in a notebook.

The butterfly's wings pulsed open and closed, displaying deep black and yellow spots on a field of orange. A tiny line of pale blue dots ran along the edge of the wings. Toby had one leg crossed over the other and waved the polished toe of his dress shoe above the butterfly's wings. It shifted away, made a little circuit of the flagstones, flying under the legs of the iron chair, then returned to the spot near Toby.

The movement had caught Michael's attention. He came over for a closer view.

"The wings are so gorgeous. Those colors are so rich. What kind is it?" I asked Michael. "Do you know?"

"*Aglais urticae*," he said. "A small tortoiseshell."

"But the body, look at it," Monique said. "It's still an insect. I don't care how nice the wings are. Look at the antenna and those creepy legs..." she trailed off as Toby moved his foot, pinning one of the butterfly's wings to the flagstone. The butterfly struggled, the other wing flailing. He released the pressure of his foot. The wings moved, the bright yellow and orange flickering in tandem, as the butterfly rose, then Toby again caught one wing under the sole of his shoe for a second. He flexed his foot, lifting it again. The butterfly synched its wings and rose a few inches. Toby brought his foot down squarely on it, squishing it into the flagstone.

"Why did you do that?" I asked, the question popping out, my disapproving tone carrying across the terrace so that heads turned our way.

Monique, her face furious, swiped up her sunglasses from the table and scraped back her chair. "Because he can."

CHAPTER 4

"*T*HE TEA PARTY BROKE UP pretty quickly after that," I said to Alex on the phone as I contemplated the three dresses Ella had put on the bed for me. I was to pick one to wear to dinner.

"He sounds like a real charmer," Alex said.

"You know, I would have said he was fairly nice until he stepped on the butterfly. Nicer than Monique, anyway. She was quite snotty. Toby tried to explain that Monique didn't like bugs and that she always had him kill them when she spotted any, but it didn't go over very well, especially with Michael."

"The bug guy?"

"Butterfly guy, specifically. He pulled out a pair of tweezers and transferred what was left of the butterfly to a tissue from his pocket."

"Hmm...I think I need a cast list."

"So do I." I looked at the pages of the packet that were spread across the desk. I'd skimmed the bios when I got back to my room and written up a set of notes for Elise, but soon it would be time to go down to dinner. From the amount of clothes Ella had laid out, it was going to take me a while. "So did you go to the ruins?"

"No. Grace didn't want to. All she wants to do is slackline." He sighed. "I put her off until tomorrow, but I can't see how walking on a flat rope beats out climbing on a ruin."

"She is on her break. Maybe in a day or two she'll want to go."

"Maybe."

Ella tapped on my door. I waved her in and told Alex I had to go. "Time to dress for dinner."

"Sounds very grand."

"It's rather intimidating, actually." We made plans to meet the next day in the gardens around lunchtime. "Maybe I can interest Grace in the maze," Alex said, his tone doubtful.

"We can try," I said saying goodbye.

"Okay." I looked over the gowns. "So it's either white, white, or white." The dresses were all made of delicate white silk, which was Regency appropriate for an evening gown for an unmarried woman, but each one had a different accent color for the sash and the trim edging the neckline and the short puffed sleeves. I had my choice of pale green, blue, and rose.

"Yes, miss," Ella said and waited.

"So…the bathroom—er, loo. Is it down the hall? I think I'll take a quick shower." I knew Parkview Hall had modern bathrooms. I'd seen them on the tour.

Ella moved to the wall of built-in cabinets and opened two of the doors, revealing a bathtub with a flexible shower head attached and a sink with a lighted mirror over it. Another door hid a toilet with the water tank mounted high over it with a dangling chain.

"How wonderful. And clever, too. It doesn't take up much space, but gives the room a private bath."

"It was added after World War One," Ella said, "but if you'd prefer, I can have a hip bath brought up. If you want to stay historically accurate."

"Bathing is the one area where I *don't* want to be historically accurate." I told Ella to come back in fifteen minutes and had a refreshing soak in the tub.

Ella returned as I was tying the cord of my cotton robe. I picked up the dress with green trim, then looked doubtfully toward the pile of undergarments. "So...how does this work?"

Ella shook out a plain cotton garment. "The chemise is first."

And it was only the first of many layers. A short corset-like garment went over the chemise, then several petticoats to give the skirt the proper flare, and then—finally—the dress. By the time I was dressed, I was beginning to understand the breach between the upper classes and their servants. It was quite humbling to strip down and then be dressed again. Servants would have seen their masters in all states—physically and emotionally, which could have been quite embarrassing. I mean, once you've seen someone naked, the relationship is definitely on a different footing. Maintaining the belief that the servants were beneath them, putting up a philosophical barrier, must have allowed the upper classes to maintain—at least in their own minds—their superiority.

Once I was laced, tightened down, then layered up, my hair was next. "It's sadly straight," I said. "It won't hold a curl longer than a nanosecond. No ringlets for me."

"I'm sure I can figure out something, miss."

As Ella brushed, combed, and twisted my hair, I watched her in the mirror. "Ella have you ever felt...uncomfortable here at Parkview?"

She took a pin out of her mouth. "I don't understand."

"Has anyone ever made...um...advances?"

"No," she said definitely. "And if they did, I'd be out of here in a flash." Her subservient manner had vanished. "There's plenty of other good jobs. I don't have to put up with that...miss," she finished, returning to her more subdued manner.

"That would be the best course," I agreed. "And Sir Harold and

Lady Stone? Do you ever see them while you're working here? Maybe on the grounds?"

"A few times. Last week, they walked with me along the drive as I was coming in to work. Lady Stone was taking her dogs for a walk, and Sir Harold was with her. He tripped and fell right against me. It was ever so lucky I was there. He could have been hurt badly."

"I see." I held out a hairpin for Ella, and she went back to work on my hair. It wasn't that I doubted Beatrice's version of the story, but I'd found that it never hurt to double check facts.

Ella finished and stepped back. She'd swept my hair up into a soft chignon fixed in place with several pins decorated with pearls. I turned my head, admiring her work in the mirror. "Wow. You'll have to show me how to do that."

Ella bobbed a curtsy and helped me into cream-colored silk shoes that looked like ballet shoes. They were a bit tight, but the material was thin and had a drawstring-type tie, so I loosened them as much as possible. How had women danced in shoes with such thin soles? I fastened my own pearl earrings on before working my hands into the gloves that went with the dress. They came up to my elbows and completed the Regency look.

I checked the mirror. "I think I'll do." I looked terrific, but with the corset, layers of fabric, and the tight-fitting gloves, I felt like a sausage.

I managed to find my way to the drawing room on my own, noticing that heavy gray clouds had rolled in, casting the corridors in gloomy light. It should have been cooler with the cloud cover, but a sticky humidity filled the air, even in the vastness of Parkview.

By the time I neared the drawing room, one of my slippers was loose and nearly flopped off my foot. I sat down in a chair with thickly carved arms and a red velvet seat near the dining room and retied the drawstring on the shoe. While I was hunched over—not an easy feat to accomplish in a corset—

Waverly glided out of the dining room and walked in the opposite direction from me, whistling softly and juggling three silver serving spoons.

I blinked, but the image didn't change. Waverly made his stately way along the hall, the spoons flashing in the light as they sailed over his head, the whistling fading as he progressed away from me.

I stood and tried out the shoe, walking a few paces, which brought me even with the door to the dining room. I paused to take in the sight. A pristine, white tablecloth covered the table, hanging all the way to the floor. Peaks of elaborately folded napkins at the center of each plate marched along the table, a mountain range of linen. Masses of silver, crystal, and china glittered in the flickering candlelight from the line of massive silver candelabras that lined the center of the table.

The curtains at the dining room's tall windows were still drawn back, and a movement at one of the glass doors on the side of the room caught my attention. A figure blocked out the view of rolling hills and distant woods. It was a man in formal Regency wear. He turned the handle slowly, stepped into the room, and lifted his phone, taking several quick photos of the table. He spotted me and came to a guilty stop, his hand holding his phone still poised in the air. White spots danced in my vision from the flash. I was surprised the butterfly guy was interested in the table setting.

"Mr. Jaffery," said a voice to my right inside the room. Both Michael and I jumped. It was Holly, still in her navy uniform, her computer tablet and a stack of folders in her arms. She had entered from one of the doors on either side of the room. Besides the door to the hall, the dining room also opened to rooms that adjoined it on either side. "Can I help you?"

"Just wanted a few pictures. For my mum."

Holly hadn't seen me, and I backed up, intending to slip away without drawing more attention, but as soon as I was out of the doorway, I turned and bumped into the solid chest of Simon Page. "Excuse me," I said.

"Lost?" he asked. "The drawing room is that way." He tilted his head, indicating it was behind him.

"No, just admiring the dining room." I stepped around him.

Simon murmured something about forgetting his phone and made for the staircase, but I noticed he also paused at the open doors to the dining room for a look.

The green and gold silk of the drawing room glowed with understated light of candles and oil lamps. The electric lights were off, and the corners of the room were in darkness. No wonder all those Regency books talked about chaperones having to keep a sharp eye on their charges. Even the far corners of the room could be used for stolen moments—no balcony needed.

The ropes that normally blocked access to the furniture had been moved, and I took a seat beside Audrey, who was wearing another more formal gown in a deep royal blue. Now that her bonnet was gone, I could see her curls were short and peeked out from under the edge of her matching silk turban. She'd gone all-out with her outfit. A couple of feathers nodded as she bobbed her head. Simon, arm seams straining on his dark cut-away coat, entered and moved immediately to speak to Sir Harold, which surprised me. They seemed to be in a deep conversation. I caught the words "kerosene" and "generator."

"You look lovely," I said to Audrey. "Another of your creations?"

"Yes, thank you, but I think Monique's dress overshadows everyone's."

Monique stood near the polished wood of the harpsichord. She wore a white silk column dress, but it was miles away from the simple lines of the dress I wore. The dress with a plunging v-neck and deceptively simple skirt was cut in a way that managed to accent her figure. Pearls and sequins must have been worked into the fabric because the dress glittered with every movement.

A pearl and diamond choker encircled her neck and jeweled combs sparkled in her elaborate mass of golden curls. She looked stunning. Beside her, Toby lounged against the harpsichord, a drink in his hand, wearing a dark cutaway jacket. The jacket was his only concession to Regency attire. He'd skipped the neck-cloth, and his outfit looked a little off as he wore a plain white shirt, open at the throat.

Monique was deep in conversation with Beth, debating a recent fashion show in Milan. Beth was again flanked by her two attendants. All three of the bridal party—I'd begun to think of them that way—wore white dresses with different shades of trim. The deep neckline and frills suited Beth's curvy figure. Torrie looked uncomfortable and kept tugging at her neckline. I wanted to do the same thing, but made myself keep my hands in my lap. Odd that during the Regency every other part of a woman had to be covered, even down to her fingertips, but a deep neckline and exposed bosom were perfectly fine. Despite all the other fabric swathing my person, I felt a bit exposed in that area.

Amanda, her petite figure looking adorable in the puff sleeves and ruffles, stood a little back from the other women in the group, her gaze fixed beyond Monique on Toby.

Toby took something, a small card case it looked like, out of an interior pocket and checked something inside it, then looked toward Amanda, catching her watching him. She turned and joined the conversation between Monique and Beth.

With a small smile, Toby watched the three women then his gaze moved around the room to me. Slowly, his smile widened as he stared. I was more aware than ever of my gown's low neckline. I gave him a perfunctory smile, then shifted to speak to Jo Funderburg, who had sat down beside me.

Jo and I complimented each other on our gowns—her gown was an exquisite turquoise silk trimmed in peach and white, and she, too, had matching feathers in her hair, but her feathers curved over her ear instead of standing up straight like Audrey's headgear. I'd read in Jo's bio that she worked in the travel industry, and we chatted about that. I learned that she lived in Miami and worked for a hotel there, managing the desk clerks. She looked up to the chandelier that glittered in the candlelight. "Nothing as luxurious as this, though."

"It is quite an amazing setting," I said. "I wonder if we'll go historical and have Mr. Woodhouse's rich food at dinner or if it will be modern food."

"Mr. Woodhouse?" Jo glanced around uncertainly.

"The father in *Emma*. The hypochondriac who was always worried about rich food and cold drafts."

"Oh, of course," Jo said quickly. She looked across the room to her husband, who was standing off to the side by himself, his hand held close to his chest. The faint glow of a screen lit up his waistcoat. She sighed. "Baseball season. Why does it have to be so long? I should have known better than to book a vacation to a place that limits digital communication. Excuse me, please." She hurried across the room, her skirt swishing.

I tactfully turned away as the Funderburgs had a muffled disagreement. "But they're in extra innings..." Jay said, his voice carrying. Jo must have won the argument because he put the phone or tablet away, and they moved to get drinks.

Michael was the last to arrive. He headed immediately for the drinks, head down, but he scanned the room until he spotted Amanda. When Michael took up a position next to the wall, Sir Harold wandered over to chat with him.

Beatrice, turned out in a purple dress with a rather alarming concoction of ribbons, feathers, and flowers threaded through her hair, joined me. "Are you enjoying it, Kate?"

"Yes, very much. It's quite an experience." I lowered my voice as I said, "Although, I've been a bit distracted with meeting everyone. And the clothes...it's been quite a learning curve. I'm afraid I don't have anything to—" I almost used the word report, but amended it since we were in a crowded drawing room and someone might overhear, "—mention."

"You've only been here a few hours. You deserve some time to settle in. As far as the clothes," she paused to push a drooping ribbon behind her ear, "I feel as if I'm at a costume party. Hard to feel like oneself when wearing clothes from another century."

I noticed that Jo had moved to join Sir Harold and Michael. "If you have a few moments, later tonight or tomorrow," I heard her say to Sir Harold, "I'd like to discuss something with you."

"Of course," Sir Harold said. "Perhaps after breakfast?"

Michael shifted away from Sir Harold and Jo then accidentally bumped into Amanda. I couldn't hear what they were saying, but I noticed that Michael wasn't ducking his head or studying the floor. His attention was focused on Amanda, who looked more attentive than I'd seen her be all day.

Torrie meandered over and joined Beatrice and me. I lifted my chin toward the pair. "It looks like Amanda has an admirer."

Torrie watched them a moment, her head cocked to one side. "Maybe. It's always hard to tell with Amanda. She plays everything close to the vest. It might be that she's just relieved to not be talking about flowers and food, or she might like him. I hope it's the second. Michael seems like the kind of guy who would treat her right."

Beatrice said, "These modern relationships are so complicated."

"Especially if the guy is married," Torrie muttered then flushed, seeming to realize she'd spoken aloud. "I shouldn't have said that. I don't know anything for sure, just that Amanda went all secretive for a while. I knew she was going out with someone, but she wouldn't tell me who or let anyone meet him. So I figured the chap had to be married. He hurt her badly, I think. She slipped up once when she was upset and said he was a manipulative bas—" she stopped and amended what she was going to say. "Ah—he was manipulative. A nice, normal, guy like Michael might be just what she needs." Torrie switched her gaze from the couple back to Beatrice and me. "Please don't say anything to her about what I said."

"Of course not," I said.

"Wouldn't dream of it," Beatrice added.

Thunder rumbled distantly as Waverly announced that dinner was served, and Beatrice went to sort out the order of precedence, which would have been much easier in Regency times when people paired off and promenaded to the dining room according to social rank, but in today's more democratic times precedence was a bit trickier, depending on how you sorted people. If it were by net worth, then Toby would certainly go first...or perhaps Beth Coleson, going by the sheer size of her engagement ring. On the other hand, if the deciding factor was social media influence, Monique clearly outranked everyone.

Beatrice arranged us, putting Monique at the head of the line with Sir Harold. Toby and Beatrice were next. I was paired with Michael at the end of the line, which didn't bother me a bit as it let me watch everyone else.

I asked Michael about his book as we promenaded. "It's an in-depth study of butterfly collectors with a focus on Victorian lepidopterists," he said then seemed glad to deposit me at my chair and escape to the other end of the table. Was he embarrassed that I'd seen him sneaking into the dining room? And why had he come in from the outside when he could have just walked in from the hall?

I was seated between Simon and Jay. Beatrice cleared her throat, and everyone looked her way. "We are leaning toward historical accuracy tonight, but not bowing to it. Just as we had cocktails before dinner, which did not happen in the Regency, we will also have some contemporary food as well as food that would have been served at a Regency dinner party."

I looked over the dishes that were already arranged on the table and was relieved to see some foods I could actually identify, including lamb, peas, and bread. "We have our version of Austen's white soup, venison, pheasant, lamb cutlets, and turbot with lobster as well as various side dishes. Gentlemen, please serve the ladies. If you cannot reach something, Thomas or John will help you." She smiled at the footmen on each side of the room. Waverly stood behind Beatrice's chair, monitoring everything, his expression blank, and I wondered if my eyes had somehow played a trick on me. Had I really seen him juggling spoons? "Remember," Beatrice said, "this is the first course, so gentlemen, you converse with the lady on your right."

Simon, his coat straining around his bulky arms as he reached for dishes, offered them to me, and I sampled most of them—research, you know, thinking that the dining experience alone would interest Elise and the viewers of the documentary series. Once we had our food and drink sorted out, he asked what I did.

"I'm a location scout."

His spoon paused halfway to his mouth. "Never met anyone who does that. Tell me about it."

It was the usual reaction when I mentioned my job, and I had the reply down pat, describing how I looked for locations for television, film, and advertising clients as I tried the white soup, which was a creamy soup flavored with some sort of meat. Probably chicken, I decided.

Aware of the etiquette of the dinner table, I turned the attention back on him and asked about his work. He told me he worked for a plastics company, but it was obvious his real passion was the "preparedness movement" because that's where he directed the conversation as soon as he was able.

As he speared a glazed carrot, Simon said, "Of course, the biggest thing we have to worry about—the thing no one seems to care about— is an EMP."

"EMP?"

"Electromagnetic Pulse, a huge burst of electricity that produces magnetic fields, which are so powerful that they wipe out the electric grid. Could be from a solar flare or from a nuclear device. With no electricity, life as we know it would be over. Everything runs on electricity now. Gas pumps, bank ATMs, streetlights, all the fancy gadgets the doctors use in hospitals, not to mention communications systems like phones and the Internet."

"I see. Sounds awful."

"Oh, it will be. That's why I'm so interested in Parkview Hall. It's good to see how sustainment worked on a large scale historically."

Thunder boomed again, sounding closer. I looked at the candles. "At least we won't have an issue if the power goes out."

"That's the idea of sustainable living. You're already prepared, no matter what comes."

The plates were cleared, and the top tablecloth was removed, revealing a second tablecloth under it. Plates and silverware were positioned again and the second course was served: turkey, chicken, roast loin of pork, and mushrooms. The more exotic choices included eggs in aspic jelly and mayonnaise of fowl, a dish of chopped fowl coated in mayonnaise and garnished with watercress and hard-boiled eggs. I ate less of this course, knowing there was still dessert to come. While I nibbled, I asked Jay if he enjoyed any sports.

"Saw me watching the game?" he asked with a half-smile. "Yes, baseball. I'm a Cubs fan," he said resignedly.

"Always hopeful, then."

"Yes, I have to be."

"It's quite a sacrifice, to come to a house party where you can't watch your games."

"Well, Jo needed to come this weekend, and I'll be able to watch the games, just not at dinner. They do have Internet here. I guess people want to experience what life was like in olden times, but with all the modern conveniences."

"Yes, I suppose so," I said, thinking of the built-in bath with a shower that I'd been so glad to find tucked away behind the floor-to-ceiling cabinets in my room. "So, Jo—I mean, Mrs. Funderburg," I corrected myself as we were all using formal address tonight, "she must be a big Austen fan."

He looked across the flickering candles and caught his wife's gaze on him. "Oh, yes. Big fan. Really big fan," he said, then concentrated on cutting his turkey, and I wondered why he sounded so stilted.

A few minutes later, the tablecloth was removed to prepare for the dessert course, which Beatrice said would be ices and fresh fruit. "Regency ices were flavored shaved ice," Beatrice explained. "The ices were a delicacy because only the wealthiest families had ice houses to store meat and ice cut from the rivers in winter."

How spoiled I was, compared to the people who had lived even a few hundred years ago. Even my tiny cottage had a freezer. I could have ice cream whenever I wanted, and if I didn't happen to have any at my house, a large variety of ice cream was only a short walk away in Nether Woodsmoor's grocery.

I glanced at Simon. "You're right. If there ever is one of those EMP things, we're all toast. We wouldn't know how to begin to survive, much less store ice and make ice cream in the middle of the summer without electricity."

"Oh, I think we could figure it out. It's amazing how ingenious people are...when they have to be."

The footman swept up the white cloth, revealing the polished wood, except for a white square in front of Sir Harold. With everything else removed from the long expanse of the table, we all looked toward the white square. For a second, I thought it was a napkin that had been left accidentally under the tablecloth when the table was laid earlier, but then I saw that it was a piece of paper with opaque tape running along the edges, holding it in place.

Block letters in a thick black marker were written on the

page, so large that even I could see the words and read them upside down from almost the other end of the table. *Evil. You can't hide anymore. Soon everyone will know.* Two arrows ran down each side of the page, pointing toward Sir Harold at the head of the table.

There was a beat of silence. When the cloth was first removed Sir Harold looked puzzled, but as he read the words, his face paled. But he was British and kept his emotions in check. He motioned to the footman who had frozen like the rest of us.

"Thomas, remove this, please"

Thomas, his hands encased in white gloves fumbled with the tape, but managed to peel it away and remove the paper.

"It appears we have a practical joker in our midst," Beatrice said. She sat rigid in her chair, but her eyes blazed with anger.

"With an inappropriate sense of humor," Toby said easily. "It's like hate mail, which I get all the time. It's a mark of success. Probably a jealous competitor, working to make you look bad."

Beatrice cleared her throat. "The dessert course, Waverly," she said, and a huge silver bowl with four arms extending out from it with small bowls at their ends was placed at the center of the table. Apples, oranges, and pears filled the center bowl, while the smaller bowls held cherries, strawberries, and nuts.

We followed her lead and ignored the note, but there was a strain in the atmosphere that hadn't been there before. Conversation limped along until Beatrice stood, signaling the end of dinner. "Ladies, let's retreat to the drawing room."

CHAPTER 5

*T*HUNDER ROLLED, SOUNDING AS IF the storm was directly overhead as I entered the drawing room with the other ladies. "Tea, I think, Waverly," Beatrice said. "I know I would like a cup. We also have coffee and other drinks, if you'd like a nightcap."

Beatrice had been more formal and correct all night than I'd ever seen her before. Her usual, almost brash, manner with its hints of good humor shining through, had been tamped down. Overseeing a house party had to be exhausting, and she was also educating all of us on appropriate Regency behavior, which had to be tiring. And then there was the note.

Torrie went to the harpsichord and began to pick out a tune. Monique and Beth took seats on either side of a piecrust table, Beth asking questions about the vendors Monique had used for her wedding. Jo and Audrey headed for a chessboard and set up on opposite sides of it.

"Thank goodness no one wants to play cards. I don't think I could handle teaching the rules of loo."

"Loo?"

"One of the card games mentioned in *Pride and Prejudice*.

Holly found the directions for how to play it online. The last group of house party guests had a woman who was a Regency expert and was shocked—shocked!—that I wasn't familiar with the game and didn't know how to teach it."

"Well, there doesn't seem to be anyone like that at this party."

"Thank goodness. I suppose I can stop going on about how things were in the Regency." Beatrice's gaze rested on Monique and Beth. "This group of guests is different from the last one. The only true Regency aficionado is Audrey."

"Yes, I think you're right. I mentioned Mr. Woodhouse to Jo, and I don't think she knew who I was talking about."

"Well, there's nothing wrong with a luxurious weekend in a country house. That is part of what we advertise. Libel at dinner, on the other hand, is *not* what we promise."

"You were right earlier. It is escalating." Instead of online accusations, the harassment had shifted to an intimate, yet public, setting with some very influential people.

"What's behind it?" Beatrice asked, shifting on the cushion and frowning at the floor. "Was it simply to embarrass Harold? Or is there something else? I can't help but wait for the other shoe to drop. Surely someone wouldn't go to the trouble of anonymous online posts and then sneaking into the dining room to plant the note unless there was more to it than an effort to humiliate Harold, because that's what happened tonight. He was hurt. He didn't show it, but I could tell. So hurt."

"Can you think of anyone who has a grudge against him? Anyone who has been angry with him?"

She rolled her eyes. "No. And I have thought about it. It's me people become upset with. Harold is off in his own world. I'm the one who makes the decisions and implements the changes. Like with the cottages, but that's died down, and I can't imagine anyone making accusations regarding Harold because I shifted a few of the cottages to holiday rentals."

"Perhaps someone is angry with you, and they're attacking Sir Harold because they know it will hurt you, too."

She considered the idea. "It's possible, but the trouble over the cottages…well, the people who were upset—it was only two or three actually, but they were extremely vocal—they have moved on, out of the area, in fact. And it's not like we evicted people from their homes. These were all people who were moving out anyway."

"Perhaps you should look into them. Find out what they're doing now, where they are."

"Perhaps." She shifted again, clearly uncomfortable. "I don't like it, checking up on people. The cottage issue is closed. We've moved on."

That was Beatrice in a nutshell: get it done and move on. "Maybe someone else moved away but hasn't moved on."

"But that can't be right. It has to be someone here, someone on the staff. That note under the layers of the tablecloths proves it. It had to be one of the staff. The process of setting the table is long and involved. Waverly and the staff began yesterday, collecting the china, silver, and linen. The tablecloths were put down this morning, and the place settings for the first course were laid this afternoon. Once the places were set, you couldn't slip a note under the cloth."

"And it was taped, too," I said, thinking that would require more than a few seconds. "I did see Michael lurking about the dining room on my way down tonight, but the note would have to be in place before the table was set. I suppose the footmen set the table?"

"Yes. And I know them all. They have all been on staff for," she paused to think, "at least over a year. And I can't think what grievance they would have with Sir Harold."

"Waverly?" I asked.

She stopped her immediate denial then said, "He's worked with us occasionally, but I don't know him well. I will check."

"I think you should check the background of all your staff, long term and temporary. See if anyone has a connection to another former employee…maybe someone who was dismissed or quit unexpectedly."

Beatrice sighed. "Yes, it looks like I will need that private investigator after all."

Waverly arrived with the tea tray, and everyone gathered around except for Jo and Audrey, who were both concentrating on the chessboard. Beatrice poured. Thunder had been rumbling as we spoke, but as Beatrice handed the teacups around a sudden tapping on the windows made us all turn. "More rain," Beatrice said. "And I thought we'd had our share for the summer."

The tapping increased as drops drummed down. With her teacup in hand, Torrie went to the window. "No archery for you, Amanda."

We all looked at her curiously. "I brought my bow and arrows with me," Amanda said almost apologetically. She lifted her shoulder and ducked her head a bit in embarrassment.

"Amanda's hobby is quirky hobbies. She's always into the most unusual things," Torrie said. "Archery, whittling—"

"And tumbling," Beth added. "She's quite a good gymnast, you know. Used to terrify me, what she'd do on the balance beam and the bars when we were in school."

Amanda said, "I don't think tumbling is an odd sport."

"Geo-cashing," Torrie went on, listing them on her fingers, "hula-hooping, skimboarding—"

"Okay," Amanda said, "perhaps you're right. Maybe I'm a little weird."

"Not weird. Unusual," Torrie said. "Unusual is good."

Amanda shifted her attention to Beatrice. "I enjoy archery, but there's not many places you can practice in London. People tend to frown on me shooting arrows at a target in the park. It sounded as if there would be plenty of room to practice here."

"Yes, by all means. We probably have something you can use

for a target. Check with Neil tomorrow. You'll find him in the old stables."

"Speaking of stables," Monique said as she sat down in a chair next to the sofa where I was seated. "Are there horses? I'd like to ride."

"We don't keep horses here, but we can arrange for you to ride. Chandford is only a few miles away. They have a nice stable and welcome our visitors."

"We'll need a private space tomorrow for our discussions," Beth said as if she was part of a treaty negotiation.

"Discussions?" Beatrice asked.

"The wedding plans," Beth said, a frown on her face. How could anyone forget she was here to plan a wedding?

"Of course. Perhaps you'd like to use the China room. It's out of the way. You won't be bothered or distracted there."

Beth said, "Yes, that would be the perfect atmosphere."

I was trying to think of something to say to Monique, but my style didn't run to haute couture, so I couldn't go there. I'd decided to ask her how she was enjoying Parkview and was bracing myself for a brusque answer when the men joined us, their voices mingling with the rain pounding down. Toby immediately moved across the room to Monique. He leaned over, one hand on his flat stomach. "Darling, let me have one of your mints."

"Indigestion again?" Monique asked without looking at him as she stirred her tea.

"A bit."

It was the first words they'd exchanged all evening, I realized. The atmosphere between them was decidedly frosty. Apparently they hadn't made up since their spat on the terrace.

"No wonder, after all that rich food." Monique removed her spoon and sipped her tea. "Too bad. I don't have any mints. I'm sure Lady Stone could order you mint tea."

So, no, they were still at odds. I was about to slip away and leave them to their chilly form of fighting, but Toby straightened.

"Never mind." He walked away and accepted a cup of tea.

As Beatrice poured out more tea, she said, "No one needs to feel obligated to stay here. You can return to your rooms and relax there, if you'd like. You can request a nightcap or snack, just use the bellpull in your room. In the morning, if you'd prefer not to be awoken in the Regency manner, which means that a maid brings you chocolate and opens the curtains for you, just inform the maid assigned to you of your preference. Tomorrow morning is at your leisure, but I will give a tour of the house, if anyone is interested. Then in the afternoon we have a variety of activities to choose from—needlework lessons, clay pigeon shooting, boating on the lake, and a garden and greenhouse tour."

Beatrice handed out the cups as she spoke, and we passed them along to everyone, not strictly Regency protocol, which probably would have had the footmen handing the cups around, but the footmen weren't to be seen—probably cleaning up all those dishes—and Beatrice seemed to have decided to shift away from strict historical accuracy.

Toby and Sir Harold appeared to have bonded. They took their teacups and moved to the side of the room to examine a landscape painting of Parkview.

Monique looked up from her tiny spangled handbag and said, "Oh, I forgot them in my room."

Beatrice said, "Shall I send for a footman?"

"Yes. I have to take my sleeping pills. I meant to bring them down with me. I simply cannot sleep in new places. Whenever we travel I must have my pills, or I don't get any rest at all."

Beatrice rose and reached for the bellpull. Waverly appeared instantly, so he must have been hovering in the hall. Monique described the medicine bottle then sat back to sip her tea, but Amanda, who was moving from one seat to another, stumbled and bumped Monique's chair. Monique's hand jerked, and tea sloshed over the rim of her cup and onto the pristine white of her gown. Monique leapt up, pulling the fabric away from her leg.

"Oh no! I'm so sorry." Amanda clasped a hand over her mouth for a second, then removed it, her face horrified. "My foot caught in my hem—are you hurt? Did it burn you? And your dress. Your gorgeous dress."

"How could you be so clumsy? This is a Ventiniti. An *original* Carlotta Ventiniti." Monique, tall and statuesque, her gold curls trembling with her anger, towered over Amanda.

"I'm sorry. It was an accident," Amanda said miserably. "I'll have it cleaned. I'll do whatever—"

"No. You can't fix this."

Toby glided between the women. "Monique, darling," he said. "It's only a dress."

She sputtered. "It's a Ventiniti—"

"Yes, you made that point. Are you burnt?"

"No. I moved my hand so that it splashed on the dress...and the chair, I suppose." She looked fleetingly toward the striped silk chair.

"Don't worry about the chair," Beatrice said. "We'll be able to clean it and most likely your dress as well. Give it to Morgan. She'll see to it. I'm hard on my clothes, she's always telling me. Ah, Waverly, thank you."

Waverly appeared, his gaze straying only briefly to the brown stain on the chair, as he held out a small silver tray with a medicine bottle and a tumbler of water to Monique.

The attention and the proffered silver tray seemed to mollify her. She swept the pill bottle off the tray, shook a pill into her hand, then downed it with a gulp of water. She lifted the pill bottle in Toby's direction. "Pill, darling?"

"No, I'll take one later," Toby said with a shake of his head.

He set his teacup down on a side table and said to Beatrice, "We'll say good evening now. Thank you for the lovely—and fascinating—dinner."

Monique shoved the pill bottle into her small evening bag, jamming it in beside her cell phone, a gold tube of lipstick, and a clear plastic container that I recognized as a package of breath mints—and it was full. I could see the little white mints through the transparent package. I made a mental note. Monique was someone you did not want to make mad. She wouldn't even give you a *breath mint* if she was angry with you.

She snapped the bag closed and swept out in a flourish of her slightly damp skirt. I had notes to write up for Elise so I departed for bed next, with the rest of the group saying goodnight behind me.

On the landing of the grand staircase, I paused to look out the tall windows at the courtyard. The rain had stopped as suddenly as it began. It must have stopped during Monique's fit—that must have been why we didn't notice the absence of the rain hammering down. The benches and trees of the courtyard were soaked, and the thunder was only a faint murmur in the distance. One of the tubs with the potted plants had cracked down the side, and dark potting soil had spilled out of the gap. The heavy rain had poured through the gap, carrying the potting soil with it. Black soil covered every inch of the courtyard.

Amanda, Beth, and Torrie joined me at the window.

"Oh, look. The rain has stopped," Torrie said. "Maybe I will be able to get a run in before breakfast." She covered her mouth as she yawned. "If I can wake-up, that is. I'm knackered."

"You did run seven miles today," Amanda said. "If I did that, I'd be dead."

Torrie covered another yawn and flapped her other hand at me as she moved along the gallery. "I'm for bed."

I said goodnight and took the opposite side of the gallery. As they made their way toward the west wing, Beth's voice floated back. "It's making me reconsider an outdoor wedding...you just can't depend on the weather. So unreliable..."

I spotted the huge display case with the butterflies and headed for it, wondering if Michael had seen it yet. I slowed down to give it a longer look now that I knew the butterflies were part of a collection that drew academics. But as I came closer, I realized the door to the room next to mine was still open. I heard Monique's voice, shrill and whiny, and resumed my normal pace. I gave the room a quick glance as I walked by, and I could see why it was called the Mahogany bedroom. The rich grain of the wood covered the walls, and I could see one hefty carved poster of the bed, which was made of the same wood.

Toby, who was lounging in a chair directly in line with the door, raised a crystal tumbler in my direction.

Monique's voice stopped abruptly, and I hurried on to my room, reaching for my key, which I had put into the frilled handbag, a reticule, that went with the dress, but I didn't need it. The door was open, a gap of half an inch between the door and the doorframe. I thought I'd closed it, but I must not have pulled it completely shut.

Next door, the Mahogany bedroom door slammed with such force that the pictures on the wall bounced then I heard the sound of a lock clicking into place. I closed my own door quietly and began the long struggle to get out of my gown. To accomplish it on my own would have required flexibility on par with a member of a Chinese acrobatic troupe, which I did not have.

After ten minutes of struggling, I gave up and rang for Ella, feeling a bit like a child—I couldn't even undress myself—but Ella played her part of lady's maid to perfection, helping me out of the layers. Once I was down to the chemise, I said, "I can handle it from here. Thank you, Ella."

"Would you like a cup of hot cocoa or warm milk sent up?"

"Thank you, no."

"Are you sure? The other ladies in the hen party asked for hot chocolate. It would be no trouble to bring you some as well."

"That's nice of you to offer, but I'm fine. In fact, I'm so stuffed I don't know if I'll be able to eat breakfast in the morning."

"What time would you like to be woken?"

I opened my mouth to say that she didn't have to do that, but then closed it. It was all part of the experience. "Seven-thirty," I said, which seemed positively decadent to me since my alarm often went off sometime around four a.m. before long days of shooting or scouting.

"Very good, Miss Sharp." Ella bobbed her curtsey and went out, closing the door.

I skipped the flowing nightgown in a lawn fabric, opting for my own comfy worn t-shirt and sleep pants. It was a relief to be out of the laced corset. My back and shoulders ached from constantly standing and sitting with proper posture. The corset and the deep cut of the dress's neckline forced me to stand up straight, something I didn't do for hours on end, as my muscles were telling me.

I curled up in bed with my laptop and got my notes down on paper while everything was fresh in my mind. The canopy's curtains draped from the ceiling and were tied off at each bed post so that occupants of the bed could close themselves in, for warmth I supposed, but I left them open. I finished and closed my laptop, then clambered out of bed to put the laptop on the desk.

I'd left the double glass doors open to catch any evening breeze, but the air was thick and still. The storm hadn't blown out the humidity. It had only increased it. Before closing the door, I glanced around the courtyard. All the other balconies were empty as was the muddy courtyard below. The light glowing from inside the Mahogany bedroom went out.

I went inside and slipped the hook and eye latch into place on both sets of doors. Despite the humidity, my room with its lofty ceiling was cool enough that I wouldn't have to sleep with the doors open to be comfortable.

I went through my nightly ablutions, then made sure both my laptop and phone were plugged in to charge, a nightly routine.

The aim for historical accuracy didn't extend fully to the bedrooms. No candlelight or gas lamps here, and all the wall outlets worked, I was happy to see as the charging icon appeared on my phone.

I crawled into bed, expecting to fall asleep right away after all the rich food and the strains of being so socially correct, not to mention having to stand up straight, but I didn't drift off. It was so very quiet.

I'd become accustomed to the nighttime sounds in my little cottage, the swish of the occasional car on the road through the village, the tree branch that brushed against the window when the wind stirred it, and the neighbor who let her dog out around ten, and invariably called for it to return, her voice carrying across the darkness.

Parkview Hall's blanketing quietness seemed loud, somehow. I almost wished I had one of Monique's sleeping pills. My mind kept going over the strange scene in the dining room. I hoped that Beatrice would get a private investigator right away. I couldn't shake the feeling that things were only going to get worse.

CHAPTER 6

I WAS SITTING ON THE balcony the next morning in the thready sunlight that occasionally peeped through the gray clouds already attired in my gown of choice, a royal blue creation in a soft cotton, drinking the cup of chocolate that Ella had brought for me while watching a man clear the mud off the courtyard with long sweeping motions of a hose when I heard a short scream, followed by the bang of a door hitting a wall, then a muffled voice in the hallway.

It sounded like Ella, so I crossed my room and opened the door. Ella stood backed against the far wall of the hallway, her eyes huge. Her complexion was nearly the same color as the white cap on her head.

"Ella, what's wrong?" I asked, anger already rising at the thought that Monique had thrown a temper tantrum and directed her anger at Ella.

"They're dead," Ella whispered with a little shake of her head. "I went to wake her. She wanted to ride this morning, so I had to go in. Mrs. King said to. She said to go in the room, and wake her then tell her the time of the riding appointment. But they're dead. Both of them." She was breathing fast, the apron covering her chest, moving with each rapid breath. "I've never seen anything like that. Never. What should I do? I should call someone, shouldn't I?"

"You wait here. I'll...check on them."

I knocked loudly on the open door as I looked around the room. The curtains, long swaths of green velvet trimmed with a gold fringe, were open. Ella must have pulled the panels back at the windows. Like my room, this room had two pairs of glass doors that opened onto a balcony, but at the moment the doors were closed. I could see the hook and eye door latches were in place.

Twin streams of sunlight fell in long bars across the emerald and gold patterned carpet to the bed. This bed was similar in design to the one in my room, but this one was on a grander scale. And instead of the curtains draping from the ceiling to the four corners of the bed like in my room, rods connected to the four posters, and velvet curtains hung from the rods. The curtains were pushed back, but I could only see vague body-shaped outlines in the gaps between the heavy fabric.

"Monique? Toby?" I called loudly. The only sound was the soft clink of the crystals on the chandelier, as it rotated slightly overhead. Suddenly, my heart was pounding. I edged closer to the bed. Toby was closest to me, his face slack. He was shirtless and one arm and shoulder were outside the covers. I didn't have to step any closer to see the odd color of his skin or the complete stillness of his chest. I gulped and realized my breathing now matched Ella's.

I took a steadying breath and moved to the other side of the bed, just close enough to see Monique. A white silk sleep mask covered her eyes, and she wore a gown with spaghetti straps in a matching material. She was flat on her back at the edge of the mattress.

Her color looked...normal. And was that...? I inched a little closer and saw her chest moving with the rhythmic breathing of sleep. Why hadn't she answered me? I touched her shoulder. It felt warm against my cool fingers. "Monique?"

I gave her a nudge. Then a harder one.

After a few second's hesitation, I pinched the edge of the sleep mask and slid it up onto her forehead. Her eyes were closed, her dark lashes splayed against her fair skin. She sighed and shifted. I leapt back as if I'd been scorched. That was when I noticed the open pill bottle on the nightstand and the empty glass beside it.

"Kate?" Ella asked. She hadn't stayed in the hall, but now stood poised in the doorway, her face still scared.

"I'm afraid you were half right," I said. "Toby is dead, but Monique is only sleeping."

"Sleeping?" Ella took a few steps into the room.

"Yes. She took a sleeping pill last night in the drawing room and it looks as though she took another one later. You better go find Lady Stone. I'll wait here until she gets here."

Ella nodded and fled. I moved to the chair I'd seen Toby sitting in last night and perched on the cushion. The light in the room changed as clouds drifted in front of the sun. The strips of sunlight faded and the room dimmed, taking on a grayish cast. I could faintly hear the sound of the water swishing across the flagstones outside. After a few seconds, Monique moved again, and I started. I really hoped she didn't wake up until someone else got here. I couldn't imagine what her reaction would be when she realized Toby was dead—and that he'd died while they slept in the same bed. No, I definitely didn't want to be around for that scene. And I was *sure* there would be a scene.

I couldn't see their faces, the curtains hid those, but I could see Toby's weirdly colored arm stretched out on the covers.

What had happened? Did he have a heart attack? A stroke? Those were the first explanations that came to mind. He'd seemed perfectly healthy at dinner, but he'd complained of indigestion. Wasn't that a warning sign of a heart attack?

I glanced at the side table where his crystal tumbler rested. There was no liquid left in it. I leaned over and sniffed. Alcohol. Scotch, maybe? I wasn't much of a drinker and wasn't sure. Had Toby washed down one of Monique's sleeping pills with alcohol? Not a good combination. An old-fashioned skeleton key lay beside the drink. It had a tassel of dark green attached to the end of it.

I hadn't met Mrs. King, but I had no doubt that the tall woman with the comfortably padded figure and disapproving frown who strode into the room was the housekeeper. The jingle of keys rang out with each of her steps. She wasn't in historical costume. She wore the navy blazer and a skirt of Parkview Hall employees with a stiffly starched white shirt and thick-soled shoes that reminded me of Grace's school uniform shoes. Ella hovered uncertainly in the doorway.

Mrs. King's glance swept around the room. She gave me a quick nod. "You'll be Kate Sharp."

"Yes, I heard Ella—"

"She told me." Mrs. King moved to the side of the bed. She paused for a moment, then swept the curtain back. The gold rings jangled loudly against the rod, but neither figure moved. Mrs. King pressed her fingers to Toby's neck for a moment, then moved to the other side of the bed and put her fingers on Monique's neck as she peered at her. Finally, Mrs. King straightened and let out a long breath through her nose. She didn't say anything, but her breathing, posture, and face radiated disapproval.

Ella had slipped in the door and crossed silently to stand beside me. She said in an undertone, "Lady Stone isn't here this morning. She's at the Lodge. Mrs. King seemed the one to go to. I hope that was right."

"You did fine," I said as Mrs. King pulled back her jacket, setting off more clinking and jangles as she moved. She removed a walkie-talkie that had been clipped to her skirt and clicked a button. "Beatrice, you're needed in the Mahogany bedroom at once. It's an emergency."

After a few seconds of static, Beatrice's voice came through the speaker. "On my way."

Mrs. King returned the walkie-talkie to her waistband. She turned to me. "Who else has been in here?"

"Since Ella left, no one."

Mrs. King shifted her gaze to Ella. "And you unlocked the door this morning?"

"Yes, ma'am. With the key you gave me."

Mrs. King gave a quick nod, then motioned to the door. "We'd best wait in the hallway."

"We should call the police," I said. "And maybe a doctor for Monique."

"We'll do nothing until Lady Stone arrives. Mr. Clay is beyond help. Mrs. Clay has a steady heartbeat and is breathing normally." She motioned toward the door.

Ella was already in the hall, but I said, "Waiting doesn't seem right."

"We have procedures. They will be put into action, once Lady Stone says to do so."

I could recognize a brick wall when I saw one, so I didn't say anything else. Beatrice arrived almost immediately. She wore a beautiful day gown in a tangerine color. She loped along the hall-way, taking giant steps, her natural stride, the fabric of the skirt snapping and flaring, her face worried. "You said an emergency?"

Mrs. King pressed her lips together and let out another disapproving breath through her nose. "I'm afraid so. You'd best see for yourself." She pointed Ella and me in the direction of an upholstered bench along the wall, opposite the case of butterflies.

If Beatrice hadn't arrived, I would have gone to my room to find my phone and called the police myself, but since she was here, I didn't. She would see they were called. I sat down beside Ella. Her color looked better, but I noticed her hands were shaking as she smoothed her apron over her black skirt. "How are you doing?"

"A little better now. I just couldn't believe it. It scared me so bad, when neither one of them moved. I know I should be examining myself, my reactions, my thoughts, for later—for parts, you know—but I can't seem to do it."

"I expect you'll remember how you felt for a long time."

She nodded. "I didn't even want to go in. It felt awkward. I know it's part of creating authenticity, making it feel like it's 1811, but I was afraid that they wouldn't like it. Having to wake someone out of a sound sleep...that didn't seem like a good idea."

"Especially when that someone is Monique," I said, dryly.

Ella gave a faint smile. "Yes, that was it, exactly. But Mrs. King said Mrs. Clay was clear—she wanted to ride, so I had to go in. Mrs. King said I could knock, but if they didn't answer straightaway, I was to use the key and go in."

"Do you have a passkey?" I asked. Her hands weren't shaking as much. Talking seemed to be calming her.

"Oh, no. I only had that key," she looked toward the door to the Mahogany bedroom, where a skeleton key with a white label on a string dangled from the lock. "It's from Mrs. King's key ring, the one she keeps in her jacket pocket. No one else has keys to the bedrooms."

"No one? Not even Bea—I mean Lady Stone?"

"No," Ella said, "It's all to do with security and the house guests. It was part of the briefing we had before the first party of house guests arrived. The locks have all been rekeyed, and only the guests have a key to their room. If they lose it, then we have to go to Mrs. King. She has the only other copy."

"But how will you get in to clean the rooms and make the beds?"

"Mrs. King accompanies us. She unlocks the doors and stays in the area until the rooms are clean. Then she locks up again. "

And inspects the results, I bet.

"It should have worked. We only have six rooms to clean."

"Six?"

"Yes, the three couples have a room, the butterfly guy has a room, the hen party ladies are sharing a room, and you. That's six. Three in this wing and three in the other wing. Mrs. King said we should be finished with the rooms before lunch, but I don't think that will happen now."

Beatrice emerged from the room, a cell phone already pressed to her ear. Mrs. King followed her, then shut the door firmly.

"Yes," Beatrice said into the phone. "Send emergency services. Can you get in touch with DCI Quimby? Oh. In that case, have them send whoever they can spare. Because it's murder, of course. Why else would I ask for the DCI?"

CHAPTER 7

"**M**URDER?" I ASKED, SHOCKED.

ELLA sucked in a breath, and Mrs. King, her face scandalized, looked up and down the hall quickly. "Beatrice," she whispered in a warning tone.

"It is, Nancy. No doubt about it. And it won't do us any good to pretend it's not. Any doctor worth his salt will recognize the signs."

"What signs?" I asked.

"Petechial hemorrhages." The medical term rolled off Beatrice's tongue. Seeing that none of us knew what the word meant, she added, "Tiny broken blood vessels in the face and eyes. He's been suffocated. You didn't notice the small red dots on his face?"

Mrs. King shook her head, and Beatrice looked to me.

"I didn't notice them either. It was dark with the bed curtains blocking the light, but if you say they were there..."

"Yes. Definite signs of asphyxiation."

"But how do you know about—I mean, surely that's not a common thing..." Mrs. King trailed off then said, "I'm sorry. It's the shock." I had a feeling that the housekeeper was in distinctly unusual territory. She didn't strike me as someone who was normally tentative or unsure of herself—or someone who questioned her employer, either.

Beatrice patted her arm. "It's fine, Nancy. I was a nurse. Before I met Harold, I trained and worked in the casualty ward. You don't forget the things you saw there."

"I see," Mrs. King said, but it was clear from her tone that she hadn't known this bit of information about Beatrice.

I hadn't either, but it didn't surprise me. I could see Beatrice treating patients with a firm, yet kind manner.

"It was a shocking disappointment to my family, of course. I did partially redeem myself by marrying Harold, though."

"What about her—Mrs. Clay?" Ella said suddenly. "What's wrong with her?"

"One too many sleeping pills, I'd say. Not much to be done for her until after the doctor sees her."

"Shouldn't someone be in there?" Ella asked. "In case she…you know…wakes up?"

"Yes, I'll wait with her," Beatrice said. "The constable will be here soon. Nancy, wait for him in the entry hall. Bring him up as soon as he arrives. I doubt it will be long. Ella, you go down to the kitchens and tell the caterer to give you a strong cup of tea with lots of sugar in it."

Ella nodded and hurried after Mrs. King, who was already striding away.

"I suppose I should wait in my room—" I broke off at the sound of fabric rustling that came from the Mahogany bedroom.

Beatrice motioned for me to follow her and strode quickly into the room.

Monique had a hand over her eyes, shielding her face from the muted light of the overcast day that filtered in through the glass doors. "Who opened those windows?" Keeping one hand over her eyes, she struggled up to a sitting position, then pulled the sleep mask off her forehead. She slammed it down on the bed and connected with Toby's shoulder. Something about it must have felt wrong to her because she froze and looked down at him, then she opened her mouth and let out a scream that I was sure resounded up and down every corridor at Parkview.

MONIQUE REFUSED to wait in the Mahogany bedroom for emergency services. She sat, wrapped in my rather worn cotton robe, her blond curls falling over her face, huddled in one of the chairs in front of the fireplace.

Her screams had brought some of the guests and several staff members. It had been a chaotic few minutes as Monique scrambled out of the bed and threw herself at Beatrice. Her bare shoulders heaving, Monique had stood with her head turned away from the bed, her white silk gown trembling with each sob.

The guests and staff had poured into the room, their questions and shocked exclamations creating a din that, at first, drowned out Beatrice's request for them to leave. The footmen and maids had followed her directions and filed out first, followed by the rest of the guests. Beatrice had maneuvered Monique out of the room. Her screams had tapered off into a series of hiccupy sobs and then silence.

I was glad to finally see Constable Albertson's familiar face. He had arrived while we were milling about the hallway, and after a quick look around the Mahogany bedroom, he had called for more officers, who gave all of us curious looks, reminding me that some of us were in period clothes.

Albertson took down everyone's name and then had sent everyone off to their rooms to wait for further instructions— everyone except Monique, who had shied away from the now closed door to her room. Beatrice had suggested Monique wait with me in the Rose bedroom. She sat with a box of tissue in her lap, dabbing at her puffy eyes, with a shell-shocked, slightly dazed manner, yawning occasionally. The medical people had examined Monique. Other than a residual grogginess, she seemed to be fine.

A rap on the door sounded, and Constable Albertson poked his craggy face around the door. "The surgeon has examined the body, and the DCI is on his way. He'll want a place to set up."

"Certainly. He can use my office," Beatrice said. "Did the surgeon indicate..." she trailed off as she looked at Monique.

Albertson glanced at Monique quickly, then shifted his shoulder so that his back was to her. "He agreed with your assessment," he said quietly.

Beatrice blew out a long breath. "I see."

Monique, tissue pressed to her nose, stared at Albertson's back. She sniffed, balled the tissue, and dropped it onto the pile on the floor beside her. "I don't understand...the DCI?"

Albertson turned to her. "Detective Chief Inspector Hopkins, ma'am."

"The police? Why?" Monique asked, her forehead wrinkling.

"To investigate. Your husband...," he cleared his throat. "The DCI will tell you."

Monique ran a hand over her eyes and fought off a yawn. "No. Tell me. What is going on?" She held out a hand to him, her face confused and lost. "Please, I have a right to know."

Albertson looked uncomfortable. "The death of your husband was...It appears there was foul play."

"Foul play? You mean...murder? No. It couldn't have been." Her curls bounced as she shook her head. "He had a weak heart, but he didn't want anyone to know. He said it would put him at a disadvantage so he kept it quiet. Very quiet." She rubbed her eyes and sighed. "Oh, I'm so tired. I shouldn't have taken that second sleeping pill. Toby told me not to, but I was so wound up." She sat up straighter and opened her eyes wide, clearly an effort to stay alert. "Only a few people knew about his heart, but that's what happened. His heart just gave out." She breathed in deeply and hid another yawn behind her hand, finally speaking around the tail end of her yawn. "So you can send the inspector chap away."

Beatrice said, "We can't do that."

Constable Albertson nodded. "The police surgeon confirmed it. It must be investigated," he said gently to Monique. Albertson turned to Beatrice. "I'll send for you as soon as the DCI arrives." The door clicked closed, and Monique focused her puffy gaze on Beatrice. "Why did he say that...about agreeing with your assessment?"

"There were certain signs...I shouldn't have said anything," Beatrice said. "I should have left it to the officials."

Monique stood and the tissue box fell at her feet. She ignored it and crossed the room to grip Beatrice's hand. "Tell me. Please. What did you see? I am—was—his wife. I should know."

Reluctantly, Beatrice said, "Tiny red dots on his face and eyes, hemorrhages. It's a sign of asphyxiation."

"Asphyx—" She turned and walked a few steps, the silky hem fluttering around her bare feet. "But then that would mean, it happened during the night." She rubbed her hand over her face, her bright red nails contrasting sharply with her pale skin. "He was fine when we went to sleep." She spoke more to herself than to us. "That means—someone came into the room..." she faltered then shivered. "It happened while I was in bed with him. I could have been murdered, too." Her hand went to the lapels of the robe. She gathered the material around her neck.

Constable Albertson tapped and opened the door. "The DCI is here. He's examined the scene, and he'd like to speak with all of you. If you'll follow me, please?"

Beatrice and I moved toward the door, but Monique only blinked. "I can't go like this." She waved at my robe.

"You can't remove anything from your room at this time. I'm sorry," Albertson said. "I'll have some clothes sent to you as soon as possible."

Monique's mental grogginess seemed to be clearing. She blew

out a little disapproving breath through her nose, but she must have decided that she wouldn't be able to move the constable because she only said, "And my makeup. I must have that as well."

"I understand," Albertson said. "My wife wouldn't be without hers either. I'll see that a set of clothes and your other items are transferred to you as soon as possible."

Monique gave a little nod, but still wasn't happy. She threw a frustrated look at me, and seemed to be on the point of asking if she could borrow something from me, but she must have decided that my clothes wouldn't be up to her standards. "Oh, very well," she said to Albertson. "I suppose that will have to do." Then she turned to me, extended a bare foot, and wiggled her toes. "Do you at least have some slippers I can wear?"

"I have sandals." I went to the closet while she moved to the dressing table and leaned over to look at her reflection. "I look awful." She rubbed her fingers under her eyes, removing some mascara smears, pushed her curls back behind her ears, then put on my sandals and followed Albertson out the door without saying thank you.

I wanted to change, too. I was still in my Regency day dress, but there was no way I could get out of my dress without help, and, with Monique sobbing in my room, ringing for Ella hadn't seemed like the thing to do.

We didn't see anyone during the long trek to the estate office. Once we arrived, Beatrice went into her office first to meet with the DCI, a rotund man with wavy black hair streaked with gray and dark black eyes. After a few minutes of waiting, I took a seat at a nearby desk, careful not to push the wheels of the rolling chair over my long skirt. Monique went to the tall windows and gazed out at the old stables and the new playground. After a few moments, she spun around abruptly and said, "This is all a mistake. Once I explain to him about Toby's heart, it will all be cleared up."

I glanced toward the closed door, which was so thick that we couldn't hear more than the faint murmur of voices. The police certainly seemed to be taking it seriously. "But the physical evidence..."

"I'm sure they're wrong." She waved her hand. "A few red dots does not add up to murder. I mean, it doesn't make sense. Why murder Toby?"

"Surely he had enemies and rivals? A businessman of his stature would have to," I said, thinking aloud.

"Of course he had, but no one who would *kill* him. It's too absurd to even consider."

"No shady business deals at all?" I asked, and she picked up on the disbelief in my tone.

She let out a short bark of laughter. "Not with the media constantly breathing down our necks. We couldn't go out to dinner without being photographed and mentioned in the gossip press. If there were any hint of Toby being associated with someone less than aboveboard, it would have been all over the news." She moved to the desk where I was seated and picked up a glossy magazine, which was folded back to an inner page. "See, here we are, two weeks ago in Mayfair. We can't even go for a walk without it being documented." She tossed the magazine down and idly plucked a postcard of the village from the computer monitor, then flicked it onto the magazine. "And why not kill me as well?" She demanded suddenly. "I was right there, too, as helpless as a...a newborn. I couldn't have fought back."

"So you didn't wake up at all? You don't remember anything?" I asked out of real curiosity. I had never taken sleeping pills and didn't know how strong they were.

"No. The last thing I remember was telling Toby to come to bed. I was so groggy at that point. The first pill didn't seem to be working, so I'd taken another." She looked toward the ceiling. "I know I'm not supposed to do that, but I always begin to feel lethargic after about thirty minutes, but it didn't happen last night. I was still furious about my dress. That's probably why.

Anyway, I took another, and it wasn't long before it kicked in. The last thing I remember was Toby turning out the lights."

"Did Toby take a pill, too?" I asked, remembering how she'd offered him one in the drawing room.

"Yes. He was just back from a trip to the States. He always takes one after traveling back, otherwise he wakes up at two in the morning."

The door opened. Beatrice emerged, and DCI Hopkins, moving lightly on his feet for such a large man, solemnly ushered Monique into Beatrice's office and closed the door. Beatrice pulled another rolling chair over and sat down beside me.

"I told him everything—all about the poison pen posts and the note last night at dinner, so if you think of anything that might help him that's related to these attacks on Sir Harold, go ahead and tell him. There's no need to keep anything back or keep anything secret now." She ran her hand over the fabric of her dress. We were both still in our Regency attire, and I couldn't help but wonder what the police thought of us, dressed up in costume at a crime scene. "Poison pen letters are one thing, but murder..." Beatrice pleated the fabric together and sighed. "It will all come out now...the accusations in the poison pen posts, but a man has been murdered."

"The DCI confirmed it?"

"Yes."

"But surely the death of Toby Clay has nothing to do with the insinuations about Sir Harold," I said.

"I'm afraid they may," she looked toward the window. "Until yesterday, the Mahogany bedroom was our room, Sir Harold's and mine."

CHAPTER 8

"YOU'RE SAYING THAT UP UNTIL yesterday, Friday, the Mahogany bedroom was your bedroom? Yours and Sir Harold's?"

"Yes. It has been for years, but after the first house party, we decided we'd like to remove ourselves a bit from the main house. We had more people arriving for this house party, and while we have many nice rooms at Parkview, not all of them are in tiptop shape, if you know what I mean. Especially since we're charging quite a significant amount for our house party guests, we want them to have the very best accommodations." She looked at the fabric of her dress where she'd been pleating it. She smoothed out the folds. "Removing to the Lodge seemed the best solution. It was set up as a holiday cottage, but wasn't booked for this weekend. By moving there, it freed up one of the nicest rooms, and would allow the servants to concentrate more on the guests."

"But if you just moved yesterday..." I didn't want to finish the sentence.

"Yes, Sir Harold could have been the intended victim."

I shook my head, not wanting to think it could be true...that someone would actually attempt to kill Sir Harold. "But he and

Toby…they're nothing alike—" I stumbled to a halt and Beatrice gave a ghost of a smile.

"I agree with you. Toby was the picture of a virile, healthy man, no matter if he had a heart problem or not, while Harold," she lifted one shoulder a bit. "Harold and I are both a bit more mature, shall we say. And I know I look nothing like Monique, but if someone crept into a dark room—and the bed curtains would have made it even darker—and simply took it for granted that the male form in the bed was Sir Harold…well, they might not have realized what had happened until it was too late."

I leaned forward. "But that is the weakness of the whole scenario. Why would someone plan to kill Sir Harold when you would be sleeping in bed with him? Surely, the…" I paused and then said the word, "murderer would know that they'd risk waking you as well."

She shook her head. "I have had some terrible back pain for the last few weeks. Dr. Hathaway says I've pulled a muscle and must not garden anymore. The only way I'm able to get any rest is on the firmest mattress we have. For the last week, I've been sleeping in the Dutch bedroom down the hall."

"Oh." I sat back, stunned, but then leaned forward. "But if you'd moved to the Lodge then the staff would know about it. They moved you?"

"Some of them, yes."

"And you were sure the person making these accusations was on staff. So if our poison pen person suddenly decided to up the game to murder, the killer would know not to attack you in Parkview itself, but in the Lodge."

She shook her head. "This is a large staff. Some people would know about our move, but not everyone."

At that moment, Holly rushed into the office area. "Oh, Beatrice. I just got your message. What can I do?" Holly asked, as her gaze skipped from Beatrice to me.

Constable Albertson reappeared in the doorway behind Holly. "Excuse me, but I need some vehicles moved."

Beatrice stood. "Of course. Holly why don't you come with me? This is Constable Albertson..." Their voices faded, and I tried to process everything that Beatrice had said. The thought that the attack could have been aimed at Sir Harold? No...surely it was the tiniest margin of possibility?

I sat for a few moments, mulling it over, my gaze fixed on the blotter on the desk in front of me, a monthly calendar, trying to work out why someone would kill Sir Harold. He wasn't a businessman like Toby, but he did have influence in Nether Woodsmoor, and someone was upset with him, as all the posts and the note at dinner last night showed. But upset enough to kill him? What would that accomplish? Revenge, I supposed. But was revenge worth the risk of being caught and convicted of murder?

Absently, I picked up the postcard that Monique had dislodged from the computer monitor. She'd dropped it with the back facing up, so I could see that there was no inscription, only a bit of tape folded over to hold it in place on the edge of the monitor.

I pressed it back into place beside a small studio portrait of a woman who looked to be in her seventies or eighties because of her lined face and gray-threaded hair. The postcard was a picture of Cottage Lane, the lane where my cottage was located. I suddenly wished I had said no to Elise, and was back in my overheated cottage, trying to work out how to bond with a prickly twelve-year-old as my biggest problem.

I would have liked to call Alex and hear his voice, get his measured and thoughtful take on the whole situation. My gaze drifted back down to the desktop blotter, and I stared at it absently, wondering if I had time to slip back upstairs and get my phone, but then a pattern of small marks on the calendar caught my attention. It was probably because I was staring at it with an unfocused gaze that I noticed the small diagonal bar, almost a checkmark, at the top left of several of the dates. Notes of times, names of people, phone numbers, and email addresses were scribbled on various squares of the calendar, but the single diagonal bars were spaced along the dates in a strange pattern.

The first mark was on the first day of the month, a Saturday. The next week only had one date ticked off, the Wednesday. The next week had two marks, on Sunday and Thursday. Then this week had Tuesday, and yesterday, Friday, marked.

It was an odd pattern. I frowned and studied the marks. Was it a work schedule? But that couldn't be it. No one worked only six or eight days a month. Maybe it was an overtime schedule, or, more likely, doodles.

The door opened, and Monique strode back into the main office. "I expect to be kept up-to-date, officer." Her fuzzy, befuddled manner was gone. Her face was still blotchy from crying, but even without makeup and in my scruffy robe, she carried herself as if she were striding down a red carpet.

DCI Hopkins watched her go, his face expressionless, then he raised his eyebrows at me. "Ms. Sharp, isn't it?"

I confirmed that was indeed my name and followed him into Beatrice's office. "This is Detective Sergeant Cannon." Hopkins motioned to a woman with a prominent jaw and tight ringlets of hair scraped back into a bun. She perched on a chair in the corner, a notepad in her hand. She gave me a brisk nod. Beatrice's papers had been removed and now the desktop, a polished wood, was empty except for a notebook and the DCI's phone.

Hopkins kept his gaze focused on his notebook as he took down my name and my reason for being included in the house party, which I gave as research for my boss, and spelled out Elise's name. Cannon took down my answers, too, but Hopkins must have preferred to keep his own notes as well. He printed in careful capital letters, his short, chubby fingers gripping his pen, reminding me of a kid in kindergarten learning his letters.

I was glad when he didn't ask for Elise's phone number

because the last thing I wanted was for her to get a call from the police about me. I'd had a little run-in with the police recently, which had nearly cost me my job, but he moved right on to asking about the discovery of Toby's body this morning. I did wonder why Detective Chief Inspector Quimby hadn't shown up as he had during the previous times when there had been a serious crime in Nether Woodsmoor. Perhaps he was on vacation.

Hopkins printed my answers, then asked, "You said several people entered the Mahogany bedroom after Mrs. Clay screamed?"

"Yes, Amanda, Beth, and Torrie arrived first, but they didn't step inside until Simon appeared behind them. He sort of pushed into the room and forced them inside as well. Michael was next, I think, then two footmen and a couple of maids, and finally, the Funderburgs. They were the last before Beatrice asked everyone to leave."

"And did everyone exit right away?"

"Yes, although Simon didn't seem to want to go. He, well, lingered is the only way to put it," I said, remembering how he'd craned his neck to see into the room, his gaze roving around every inch of the room until the last second.

"It made you uncomfortable."

"No, it was just...odd."

"And what was your opinion of the Clays?"

"I'd just met them," I said.

"Nevertheless, Lady Stone says you have good instincts. What did you think of them?"

It would be too catty to say Monique behaved like a spoiled brat.

Hopkins raised his eyebrows, the most expression he'd shown during the whole interview. "Come now, Ms. Sharp. I need to know what their interactions were."

"They didn't seem happy. She threw a fit when Amanda

caused her to spill her tea on her dress. Toby tried to smooth it over, but there was tension between them. Monique and Toby, I mean."

Hopkins bent over his notebook again, and I wondered if I should mention the poison pen posts, but his phone rang. He listened for a moment, then told me I could go with the phone still tucked under his ample chin. He was waiting for me to leave before he spoke again, so I opened the door and slipped out.

Holly was bent over the desk where I'd been sitting. She was rummaging through the drawers. She pulled out an older model flip phone from the back of a drawer and spotted me as she closed the drawer. "Oh, Kate. I didn't know you were in there."

"Sorry. DCI Hopkins is still in there, on the phone."

"Oh. Good to know." She snatched up her computer tablet and tried to slip the flip phone into her jacket pocket under cover of the tablet, but the phone caught on the edge of her pocket, and she had to force it inside. "So," she said brightly. "Can I help you find your way back to one of the main rooms? I'm afraid most of the activities have been canceled today, but a cold lunch is being served on the terrace."

"Lunch already?" I asked, looking at my watch. It was nearly noon.

"Yes. Let me take you there," she said and motored away.

I caught up with her, and we moved along at a furious pace, the skirts of my dress swishing and flapping. "We'll take the servant's corridor. It's much shorter." She pushed through a door at the end of the hallway. The transition was immediate. Instead of silk-covered walls, decorative furniture, and paintings, this hallway had bare walls and a plain wooden floor.

"So what has happened? Are the police still working in the Mahogany bedroom?" I asked, wondering if I could even get to my room to change.

"Yes. They've blocked off the entire wing and won't tell us when they'll be done. Here we are." She opened another door, and I followed her into the hallway near the drawing room. She moved across the tile floor to a set of glass doors. The doors led to a paved walkway that ran around the outside edge of the house. We passed the dining room, and I realized this must have been the path that Michael had taken when he came into the dining room before dinner last night. The path ran around an outcropping of the building to the smaller terrace where long tables piled with food sat in the shade near the house.

Gray clouds dotted the sky, and a cool breeze swept across the terrace, fluttering the tablecloths. The humidity had evaporated, and the sun was shining between the patches of clouds. Beth, Amanda, and Torrie sat at a café table, stacks of glossy magazines and several notebooks almost crowding their plates off the table. Audrey sat alone, wearing another beautiful Regency gown, her e-reader propped up next to her plate, a jarring counterpoint to her Empire waist dress and bonnet.

Michael, who had opted out of Regency attire, was in line for food, and I stepped behind him, but my gaze followed Holly as she nearly sprinted through the tables and trotted down the stairs to the formal gardens. The sound of a ringtone trilled, and she quickly removed a phone from her blazer pocket, but it wasn't the flip phone. She pushed a button on a sleek smartphone encased in a hot pink cover and pressed it to her ear as she walked.

The faint click of a camera shutter pulled my attention back to the buffet table. Michael was hurriedly tucking his phone into a pocket of his cargo pants. He grabbed a plate and served himself cold cuts, cheese, and bread.

While I waited for him to move along the table, I glanced over my shoulder. Holly was moving through the formal gardens rapidly. Her bobbed hair swung out from her head as she checked behind her a couple of times. The lawns were soaked after the rain last night, and she kept to the gravel paths until she reached the end of the formal gardens. Her movements were quick and sharp. She wasn't on a leisurely stroll. After another quick look around, she darted to the side, disappearing behind a tall hedge that enclosed the maze. She obviously didn't want anyone around her. What was she up to?

"Kate," a voice called, and I turned to see Alex crossing the terrace with Grace trailing along behind him. Her face was blank, but her head tilted back as she took in the imposing façade of Parkview Hall. Her gaze skipped back and forth over the architectural details of the triangular pediments over the windows up to the alternating statues and gold-edged urns perched on the roof.

"Alex," I said. "I'm so glad to see you."

"You look extremely fetching—" He broke off as soon as he stepped out of the sun and into the shade of the terrace and saw my face. "What's wrong? Can't get away for a little bit? It's fine. Grace and I can explore the maze on our own."

"No, it's fine," I said. "I just completely lost track of the time."

Grace rolled her eyes, and I thought I heard her say, "It figures." She drifted to the stone railing and draped herself over it, peering down into the formal gardens below.

I said to Alex in a low voice, "There's been a death—one of the guests. A murder." I glanced worriedly at Grace. She spun toward me and stared, all attention, every trace of lethargy gone. I didn't want to upset her, but there was no use trying to hide the news from her. I was sure it would be all over the village soon. In fact, I was surprised that she and Alex didn't already know about it, but it was obviously news to both of them because Alex was shocked.

"I wanted to call you," I said to Alex, "but they won't let us back in our rooms, and that's where my phone is. I could have used the one in Beatrice's office, but with being interviewed...I completely forgot."

Alex blinked. "A murder? Are you okay?" His face was concerned, all his concentration zeroed in on me.

"I'm fine. Well, I think we were all in shock, at least a little bit, this morning. It's not something you expect."

Grace found her voice. "A murder? Brilliant. All the girls will be jealous when I tell them. This will be just like *Sherlock*. Who was it? Did you know them? Had you talked to them? And, are those little cakes down at the end of the table? Could I have one, do you think?"

I glanced at Alex and suppressed a smile. So much for worrying about her delicate sensibilities. "Yes, help yourself. I'm sure Beatrice won't mind."

Grace quickly worked the length of the table, coming away with a plate layered with meat, cheese, and bread as well as a pile of fresh fruit and several squares of cake. Alex and I followed her, making more moderate choices.

"Let's go down here." I moved to the café table at the end of the terrace. We sat down, and I told them it was Toby Clay who had died, apparently asphyxiated during the night.

Alex choked, then swallowed. "Toby Clay?"

Grace said matter-of-factly, "Kind of like *4.50 from Paddington*," then frowned. "No, that was strangulation, not suffocation."

"What are you talking about?" Alex asked, a concerned frown on his face.

"It's an Agatha Christie book," I said. "You like classic mysteries?"

"Sure," she said with a shrug. "The school library has tons of them. Sherlock Holmes is good, too," she added then polished off several sandwiches before moving on to the cakes. At least the news hadn't scared or worried her...or affected her appetite.

Alex chewed a moment, then swallowed. "That's unfortunate —for Beatrice and Sir Harold—that it was Toby Clay. The publicity."

"Yes, I know. That's not all they have to worry about...never mind," I said, deciding that I shouldn't talk about the poison pen posts in front of Grace. I tried to make a face that expressed *I'll tell you later* to Alex, but I was new to this silent communication thing, and he just frowned at me. I shifted my gaze to Grace, who was licking icing from her fingers, and his face cleared. "Grace, did you know there's a telescope at the end of the terrace, mounted on the stone railings?"

"No, I didn't. Cool. Can I go look?"

"Sure." She scraped her chair back with a screech and was out of earshot in a few seconds. I told Alex about the posts, the note at dinner, Beatrice's suspicions about the staff, and how Sir Harold was the usual occupant of the Mahogany bedroom.

He made a low whistling sound. "What do the police think?"

"I have no idea. Quimby didn't show up. It's DCI Hopkins, and he's got the best poker face I've ever seen."

"Play a lot of poker, do you?"

"Constantly." I grinned at him. I was so serious all the time, I needed a little absurdity in my life.

A movement, something pale against the canvas of the surrounding green landscape caught my eye. I squinted. "I think that's Holly," I murmured.

"Who?"

"She's the publicity person here at Parkview," I said. "See that woman with the blond hair, moving beyond the maze up to the tree line? That *is* Holly." I recognized the short cropped haircut and her navy blazer and skirt. The land rose above the maze to a ridge, and it didn't look like it was easy walking in her pumps, but she crossed the ground at almost a run as if she didn't want to be in the open too long. "She was acting strange earlier today. Very nervous."

The artificial lake and the folly were beyond the ridge, but she didn't disappear over the ridge. Instead she picked her way through the dense trees, moving farther away from the house. Her blond head was barely a speck at this distance, but it was a bright counterpoint to the shadows under the trees. Suddenly, her head dipped toward the ground.

"Did she fall?" Alex asked.

"I can't tell." I hopped up and crossed to the telescope. "Grace, do you mind if I have a look?"

"No, go ahead. You can see all the way down to the river."

I swiveled the telescope toward the woods and squinted through the viewfinder.

It took me a few seconds to find her, but when I did manage to get the telescope aimed directly at her and focused, an image popped into clear view. Holly squatted near the ground, a palm-sized stone gripped in one hand. She brought the stone down on another rock firmly several times. I could faintly hear the sound of stone striking stone ring out. Her face was strained, and she glanced around a few more times, checking the woods between the blows.

I moved the telescope lower and focused. A crushed and mangled mess of plastic leapt into view for a second before her hands swept it up. It was mostly pieces, but I did recognize the hinge of a flip phone.

A blur of navy filled the lens, and I pulled away from the eyepiece. I scanned the woods in the distance and didn't see anything for a few moments, then I saw a flash of movement and adjusted the telescope. Holly moved to the edge of the trees at almost a run, then slowed as she cleared the woods. She went directly to the edge of the river that cut through Parkview's estate and threw the bits of plastic and metal into the swiftly moving stream.

CHAPTER 9

"*I* WISH THERE WAS SOME way I could find out more about Holly," I said to Alex. We were standing on one of the gravel paths that wound through the countryside and back to the village. It also happened to run along the stream downriver from where Holly had tossed her handful of useless electronics. Grace was trying to skip a stone across the water.

I threw out my arm and flicked the stone, trying to imitate Alex's effortless tosses that sent his rocks dancing across the water. My stone plopped into the water and disappeared.

"I mean, her history, or, well, really anything about her. It's quite a big step to go from destroying a cell phone—an old one, at that—to murdering your employer. And she has such a bouncy, perky disposition. I can't imagine her posting those nasty things about Sir Harold, much less..." I glanced toward Grace, who didn't seem to be interested in what I was saying, but amended what I'd been about to say, "anything violent."

"But she is acting suspiciously," Alex said, matching my quiet tone. He released a stone with a relaxed swing of his arm. It hopped across the water four times before sinking. "I think you should tell Beatrice and the DCI what you saw. And, I wish you'd come back to your cottage. There's no need for you to stay here. I'm sure you have more than enough details for Elise."

I agreed with him. I did need to tell Beatrice and Hopkins about Holly's actions, but I wasn't about to leave Parkview. "But there's Beatrice to think of as well. I'm not going to go off and leave her when she doesn't know who she can trust. I mean, imagine if you suspected someone you worked with was out to get you—how difficult would that be?"

"Sounds like a typical film set," Alex said with a smile, and I rolled my eyes.

The smile dropped off his face. "So what are you going to do?"

"I'll try and convince her and Sir Harold to stay at the Lodge until the DCI sorts out what has happened."

"I doubt you'll have any success. She's a tough old bird and Sir Harold is too, for all his vagueness. In fact, she's about as obstinate as you so you'll have no luck there."

I opened my mouth to protest, but he held up a hand. "And I mean obstinate in the most flattering way. You're loyal and focused."

"Well, as long as you mean it in the nicest way possible, I'll let it go." I tossed another stone, flicking my wrist for all I was worth. It sank. "You're probably right about Beatrice and Sir Harold. They won't want to leave." I selected another stone. "I could call you every hour on the hour, if it makes you feel better."

He checked his watch. "Time hack. Two-thirty. If I don't hear from you by three-thirty, I'm storming the castle."

"I'd expect nothing less."

"Come on, you two," Grace called. "There are better stones down here."

"I have to go back," I said, hating to spoil the atmosphere since Grace seemed to be actually enjoying herself. "It was good to see you both."

Alex caught my hand and pulled me close for a quick kiss

then said, "Call me tonight before you go to bed and in the morning. No joke."

I kissed him back. "I will."

"Good. I'll ask around about Holly in the village. Louise might know something. What is Holly's last name?"

"Riley. Holly Riley. Yes, if anyone knows something it will be Louise. Don't look so worried. I'm not in any danger. I'm not sleeping in the Mahogany bedroom or receiving poison pen notes."

I RETURNED TO THE HOUSE, letting the cool air in the hallway wash over me. Despite the breeze, it had been warm outside in the sun, and I felt sticky and hot from my walk. I'd entered the house through one of the entrances on the ground floor, the floor with the kitchens and storage rooms. In short, the rooms where all the work was done. I knew about the entrance because Beatrice had brought me this way the first time I'd visited Parkview. As I pushed open the door to the kitchen, sounds of conversation, laughter, and a smattering of applause rang out. When I stepped inside, the room went silent.

Several maids and footmen were seated at a long wooden table, which was filled with plates and glasses from their lunch. Some of the footmen had removed their powdered wigs and hooked them on the back of their chairs. Waverly stood at the end of the table with his arms held out straight on each side, his head tilted back toward the ceiling. The end of a long stick was balanced on his forehead. A plate spun merrily on top of the stick.

Still holding his position, he slued his gaze my way. Once he saw me, he reached up and removed the stick from his forehead. The plate kept rotating as he straightened then he gave the stick a little toss, and the plate arched over his head. He caught it with his left hand. "How can we help you, Ms. Sharp?" he said, deadpan.

"Impressive." The staff, who had been watching me tensely, seemed to relax a bit.

"Thank you, Miss Sharp." He placed the plate and stick on the table. "A little party trick. Shall I show you the way to the main floor?"

"I'm actually looking for Holly. Do you know where she is?"

"I believe she's left the estate for a few hours on an errand. Can I help you?"

"I need to speak to her…it's for the Jane Austen documentary series that I'm here researching," I added. It would be perfectly logical to talk to the publicity person about the documentary. "It's a bit urgent. She hasn't gone home for the day?" I asked, just to make sure she was coming back.

"I don't believe so," Waverly said.

"If she did leave, she lives in Upper Benning with her gran," one of the maids offered as she pushed back her chair and began to gather plates. "I take the same bus." She glanced at the clock. "There won't be another until five-thirty this evening, then after that, there's one more at ten."

"Since Holly is gone, I better speak to Beatrice. I mean Lady Stone."

Thomas stood. "She's with the DCI."

"Will you let her know I need to speak to her as soon as she is free?"

"Yes, miss." Thomas shoved his wig on his head and moved away from the table.

"But you can finish your lunch first," I said.

"We're done," Thomas said. "We were just having a bit of fun. Mr. Waverly was showing us some of the things he learned when he was in the circus. He was a magician and had his own act—" Waverly caught Thomas's eye, and Thomas stopped speaking. "I'll deliver that message." Thomas slipped out the door.

"Can I escort you to the main floor, Ms. Sharp?" Waverly intoned, all formality.

"No, I can find my way. Sorry to interrupt."

I left the kitchen and made my way upstairs to the east wing. I was relieved to see that the wing wasn't blocked, and, only the door to the Mahogany bedroom had crime tape over it.

I unlocked the door to my room, intending to ring for Ella to help me get out of the period dress, but when I stepped inside my room Simon came through the doors from the balcony.

I stopped short. "What are you doing in here?"

"Sorry." He held up a hand. "I know I shouldn't be poking about in your room, but true crime is a bit of a hobby of mine. And I went straight to the balcony. Didn't touch anything in your room."

"I thought prepping was your hobby." I had automatically pushed the door closed as I went in my room. I backed up a few steps until I felt the door at my back.

"A bloke can have more than one hobby, can't he?"

"I suppose so. I'd like you to leave." I opened the door and motioned toward the hallway.

"Out of curiosity, did you hear anything last night? Maybe out on the balcony?" He crossed his beefy arms and made no move to leave.

"No." I wasn't about to tell him anything. I just wanted him out of my room.

"Did you go out there...or next door to the Mahogany bedroom?"

"No." If he wasn't leaving, then I was. But as I stepped into the hallway, he shot across the room, moving surprisingly fast despite his heavy build, and caught my arm just above the elbow in a tight grip. He pointed a flat and rectangular box at me.

"If you behave, I won't have to use it."

"Use it?" I shrank back.

His viselike grip tightened. "It's a stun gun. No need to look so scared. It's just a little shock. It won't hurt you. It will only make sure you stay put until the police arrive."

"Yes, the police sound like an excellent idea. Let's call them."

"Oh, I intend to. They'll be interested to talk to you. You'd be wise not to lie to them, like you did to me just now."

"Lie to you? What are you talking about?" He wasn't making sense, but at least he wanted the police. So much for my worries about Holly acting strangely. This was much, much weirder.

Had he sent the poison pen notes and murdered Toby? I decided those details didn't matter at the moment. "Let's get the police here. I'll call them, if you like."

He snorted. "Oh no. I'm not that gullible. I'll call them myself." He steered me back into the room. I wanted to move the opposite way, out into the hall, but he was too strong and propelled me across the room, then shoved me into one of the chairs in front of the fireplace. He held the stun gun inches out of my reach. "Don't try anything." He pressed a button, and an electric current arched between two posts as he backed up a few steps and yanked the bellpull.

"I wouldn't dream of it."

After a few tense minutes, Thomas appeared in the open doorway and, even with his training, couldn't keep his expression impassive. "Blimey." Doubt chased across his face and was quickly replaced by determination. He tensed.

"Thomas," I said, afraid he was about to charge Simon. I didn't want Simon discharging the stun gun while I was anywhere in its vicinity. "Would you get the DCI and Lady Stone?" He didn't move, clearly unsure what to do. "Quickly, please," I added, trying to achieve a tone worthy of a commanding Regency lady, but my voice was breathy, which spoiled it a bit.

He licked his lips, then nodded and departed at a run.

I could suddenly hear the ticking of a clock from down the hall and the twitter of a bird through the open door to the balcony. My phone, which was still plugged into the outlet, rang. I could see from the display that it was Alex.

Simon shook his head. "Don't move."

I bit my lip as the ringing continued until the chime rang out that indicated the call had been sent to voicemail.

I heard Thomas's voice. "...last room on the left." And then DCI Hopkins's large frame filled the doorway. Relief washed over me, and I realized I was gripping the arms of the chair.

Hopkins looked from Simon to me then said, "Mr. Page, suppose you let me have that?" He held out his hand.

"Not unless you're armed," Simon said. "We don't want her to get away."

"I'm sorry?" Hopkins leaned forward, a single frown line creasing his brow.

"She's dangerous. She's the murderer."

CHAPTER 10

"*I*S SHE?" HOPKINS SAID, MILDLY. "The stun gun, Mr. Page," he added in a firmer voice.

With one last look at me, Simon handed over the stun gun. Hopkins checked it and pushed a button. Because the current didn't arc, I assumed it was a safety pin. He put the stun gun in an interior pocket of his jacket. "Now, suppose you tell me why you think Ms. Sharp is the murderer." He motioned Simon toward the matching floral chair beside me. Simon didn't look as if he wanted to take a seat, but Hopkins exuded authority, which is why I suppose that Simon gave up the stun gun. Hopkins nodded to the chair again, and Simon took a seat. Hopkins picked up the dressing table chair and placed it squarely in front of the fireplace, creating a conversational triangle—a *tense* conversational triangle.

Hopkins balanced his bulky frame on the little chair. "Mr. Page." Hopkins waved a hand, indicating Simon should speak.

"She's been on the other balcony, the balcony to the Mahogany bedroom. She denied it."

"Is that so?" Hopkins looked toward me.

"No, of course not. I have been on *my* balcony, but how would

I get to the other one?" A gap of several feet separated the balconies.

"It's not that large of a distance," Simon said. "A person could cover it, if they stretched or jumped."

I looked at Hopkins. "That's crazy. Who would do that?"

"The murderer did." Simon cut in before Hopkins could speak. "There are only two keys to each guest room. The guest has one, and the housekeeper has the other." Simon paused and said as an aside to Hopkins, "Security is important to me. I asked about this when we arrived."

Simon looked back at me. "The maid, Ella, said she unlocked the door to the Mahogany bedroom this morning with the key from the housekeeper—I asked her—and I saw the other key on the table inside the room. Therefore, the room was locked. The murderer *had* to enter from the balcony. You are the only person with access to the balcony. Only your room and the Mahogany bedroom have balconies on this wing of the house. It's the only explanation. You went in through the balcony and suffocated Toby Clay."

"But I didn't climb over the balcony or go anywhere near Toby Clay last night. How can you even think that?"

Simon smiled like he'd just won a prize, displaying the slight gap between his two front teeth. "There. She did it again," he said to Hopkins. "She's lying." Simon settled back in the chair and crossed his thick arms as he looked at me. "That's how I know you did it."

"Do you have proof of your accusations, Mr. Page?"

"Yes. Her hairpin is on the balcony...the balcony to the Mahogany bedroom. Your men must have missed it. It's under the flower pot thing. It's difficult to see it, but it is definitely there. It's just like those on the little table there." He pointed to the dressing table. I swiveled and saw the stack of hairpins that Ella had used to put up my hair last night.

"That's why I was in here," Simon said. "I wanted to check the balcony. With the other room sealed off, your room was the only way I could see the balcony."

"And how did you get in here?"

"The door was open."

I frowned. Had I left the door open? I couldn't remember. In all the confusion with the police arriving and Monique's crying jags, I might have. How Simon got in my room was the least of my worries. "This is absurd," I said, looking at Hopkins. Surely he didn't believe Simon?

"Go and look," Simon said confidently. "It's there on the other balcony. And before you say that it could have belonged to anyone, my wife noticed those pins last night and asked our maid about them. The maid said that the hairpins were part of the costume that's provided for the guests. Each female guest had a different set. There was only one package with those pearl things attached, and she said that your maid used them all in your hair."

I jumped up and went to the balcony, skirting around Simon.

I didn't see it at first, but when I bent down and peered through the stone balusters to the balcony of the Mahogany bedroom, I saw the soft glow of a pearl attached to a hairpin almost hidden under the edge of the ceramic pot that held the boxwood shrub.

"I did not leave that there." I stood and bumped into Hopkins, who was right behind me. I sidestepped and moved to go around him.

"Please." He caught my wrist before I touched the back of one of the chairs. "Fingerprints."

I snatched my hand back, and he pulled out his phone. "One moment." He made a call, instructing someone to photograph the hairpin, collect it as evidence, then dust my balcony for prints. He put his phone away. "We have already checked that balcony for prints," he said, tilting his head toward the Mahogany bedroom balcony.

I felt myself go cold. Hopkins was taking everything that Simon had said seriously.

Simon was on the balcony, too. He pointed to the hairpin. "I think she pried the hairpin open. See how it's bent back? She was able to get it between the glass doors and force the latch open. These doors are only held closed with these hooks." He flicked at one of the hooks that dangled on the glass door of my balcony. "It would only take a little force to get the hairpin through the slight crack—these doors don't close completely. Old house, you know. Add some upward pressure, and it would push it out of the 'eye' where it usually rests."

"But the balcony doors were locked when Ella found Toby Clay dead this morning," I said. "I noticed it because Ella had pulled back the curtains to let in the light. How could someone... not me, because I didn't do it," I said firmly, "...how could someone relatch them if they entered and left through the balcony?"

"Simple. You relatched them after the body was discovered this morning. You were alone in the room, weren't you?" Simon said, his voice soft, but his expression was triumphant. "Ella said you were. She said you told her to fetch help and stayed there alone. You had plenty of time to relatch the hook."

Stunned, I could only shake my head for a moment, then common sense swept back in. "Well, then why didn't I throw away the hairpin or at least remove it?"

"You either didn't have time, or you couldn't reach it. It is on the far side next to the row of balusters. It would be hard to get to."

"Then why leave it in the first place?" I asked recklessly.

"You would have lost it last night. Probably dropped it after you got the door unlatched. It was dark," Simon said, answering my question seriously. "You probably didn't want to use a light for fear of attracting attention. You probably dropped it, couldn't find it, and hoped it had gone over the edge."

I blinked at him a moment and decided to cut my losses. Simon clearly thought he'd worked out a way that I'd murdered Toby in a clever, convoluted way, and he wouldn't even consider any argument I made. I turned to Hopkins. "He's completely wrong. I have not been on that balcony," I said. "I don't know how that hairpin got there, but I certainly didn't put it there."

"So you were in this room all of last night?" Hopkins asked. He gestured for me to precede him into the room, and I walked back inside on legs that were suddenly shaky.

"Yes."

"Alone? No one else can verify that?"

"No. Of course I was alone. I don't have a companion this weekend. Who else would be able to verify that?" I asked, my voice rising.

"Please, Ms. Sharp. These questions, must be asked." He looked at Simon, who had followed us into the room. "And you, Mr. Page. Where were you last night?"

"Me?"

"Yes."

"I'm not the one under suspicion here. In fact, Sir Harold hired me to look into a few things for him."

"Did he? What sort of things?" Hopkins asked.

Simon frowned and looked as if he didn't want to say anything, but then reluctantly said, "I suppose you'll have to know. Sir Harold hired me to find out who was saying some rather unsavory things about him."

"Why would Sir Harold hire someone who works in a plastics company?" I asked.

Simon pulled at the collar of his polo shirt that hugged his large neck. "Fact is, that was a cover story. I'm a private detective."

Hopkins said, "I'll need to see your license."

Simon removed a card from his wallet and handed it over.

"What about Audrey? Is she undercover, too?" I asked. "Is she even your wife?"

Hopkins looked inquiringly at Simon.

"Yes, of course she's my wife. One and only time that she's gone on a job with me. Sir Harold invited her as well, said we'd blend in better if we were a couple. Audrey was over the moon when she found out it was a Regency weekend."

"How did Sir Harold come to hire you?" Hopkins asked.

"I met him on the train last week up from London. We chatted. When he found out what I did, he explained the problem they were having and invited me to come to help sort it out."

"And where were you last night?" Hopkins asked.

Simon looked offended. "In my room. With my wife. All night."

"Very good." Hopkins had removed his notebook and printed Simon's answer. "If you'll both take a seat again. I have a few more questions." Once we were seated, Hopkins said, "You look bemused, Ms. Sharp."

"I am. Beatrice asked me to come this weekend to do the same thing Mr. Page is doing...to figure out who was sending these poison pen posts about Sir Harold."

Simon looked incredulous. "That can't be. Why would she do that when there was a real private detective on the job?"

Perhaps she knew the caliber of your detecting skills, I thought, but managed not to say aloud. "Sir Harold is a bit forgetful and vague at times. He may have simply forgotten to tell her that he'd hired you." Simon looked even more offended. "And Beatrice is not one to wait around for someone else to do things. She probably asked me to come this weekend and didn't know about your double role."

"And why would she ask *you*?" Simon asked. Hopkins looked interested, too, and I felt a little uncomfortable, but there was nothing to do but get it out in the open.

"There have been a couple of times when I noticed a few

things that were relevant in police investigations. Beatrice thought I might notice something this weekend."

"So you're *not* a location scout," Simon said, his tone triumphant. "There's another lie."

"Mr. Page," Hopkins said, warningly.

"No, I am," I said. "And I am here to research the possibility of using one of these country home weekends as a short feature in a television documentary. The two things—the research and keeping an eye out for Beatrice—just dovetailed nicely, timing-wise."

Hopkins cleared his throat. "Back to the hairpin."

I felt my insides sink. We were back to that.

"Did you remove your hairpins last night or did the maid," he consulted his notes, "Ella, do it?"

"No, I did it myself, and I left them there on the dresser. I haven't touched them, but if the door was open," I glanced at Simon, "anyone could get in here and pick one up."

"And you stated," he paused and flicked the pages of his note-book backward, "the glass doors to the balcony were locked this morning when you entered the room next door?"

"Yes, but surely there are other ways to get into the room? Perhaps there is a third key to that room, or maybe someone repelled down from the roof."

I gave a little half-laugh as I made the last statement, but Hopkins said, "No, that is not a possibility," his tone serious. "Parkview has closed circuit cameras mounted on the roof—helps them with maintenance, it seems. Constable Albertson reviewed all the footage, and no movements or activity were recorded on the roof during the night. Likewise, the hallway is under observation. No one entered or left through the hallway door after the Clays retired for the night. The first person to enter was the maid at eight-ten."

"Oh," I said, optimism whooshing out of me. I felt like a deflated balloon that sags near the ground a couple of days after a party. "And the courtyard? Are there cameras there, too?"

"No," Hopkins said, a shade of disappointment shading his voice, "but the groundskeeper tells me one of the shrubbery enclosures cracked open and the heavy rain washed most of the soil out of the enclosure, which completely covered the flagstones. Since it didn't rain again during the night, anyone crossing the courtyard would have left footprints in the soil, and there were none this morning when one of the groundskeepers hosed down the courtyard."

I closed my eyes and leaned back. I had looked down on the courtyard this morning myself and seen the coating of unmarred soil on the flagstones. At the time, I'd simply thought *what a mess —glad I don't have to clean up that mess.*

"We have the testimony of several witnesses that the soil was undisturbed this morning."

"Yes, it was."

Hopkins closed his notebook. "The classic locked room mystery, it seems."

CHAPTER 11

*H*OPKINS TUCKED HIS NOTEBOOK INTO his jacket pocket. "Of course, despite the seeming impossibility of the crime, there's always an explanation."

That was true. There had to be an explanation. "Since I know I didn't climb over the balcony and get into the Mahogany bedroom, you'll have to look for another explanation. Is there a servants' entrance?"

"No. The servant staircase is at the end of the hall. No passages connect directly to any of the bedrooms."

"An air vent?" I was reaching, I knew, but it was all I could think of.

"None that would be large enough for a person to crawl into."

"Well, what about Monique? She was actually in the room with him. Isn't she a suspect?"

A corner of Hopkins's mouth twitched. "You're persistent, I'll give you that. Normally, I wouldn't share this information, but," he narrowed his eyes and studied me then gave a small nod, "yes, I think you are the type who will hound my people, preventing them from doing their work and generally interfering, so I will tell you that the medical team who examined Monique Clay this morning confirmed that her vital signs and physical appearance were consistent with the ingestion of a greater dose of sleeping pills than would be prescribed for her."

I opened my mouth, but Hopkins held up a hand. "Her bottle of sleeping pills was a new one and contained the exact number of pills that it should contain. Three were missing. She says she took two and that her husband took one, a usual occurrence, she says."

"So she actually slept through the night and wasn't aware of... anything?" I asked.

"That is the opinion of the medical personnel who examined her this morning." Hopkins watched me with his blank face. I had no idea if he thought I might actually be a murderer, or if he thought Simon's accusation was complete garbage—but there was the hairpin, my hairpin, on the balcony. He wouldn't be able to discount that. He'd have to investigate.

"Look," I said. "I'd never met either Toby or Monique before yesterday. I have no reason to want to break into their room or harm Toby in any way, but I do know that Holly Riley has been acting odd today. Perhaps you should look at the staff instead of focusing on access to the room. The death might be tied to the poison pen posts. Beatrice thinks someone on staff was responsible for those. And with the Mahogany bedroom being Sir Harold's usual room..."

Simon said, "That would be convenient for you, wouldn't it? Take the attention off you."

Hopkins' eyebrows drew together producing a wrinkle. "Holly Riley, the publicity director?"

"Yes, that's right."

"What odd behavior have you observed?"

"She went into the woods today, crushed a cell phone with a rock, then threw the pieces into the river." There was a second of silence as both men processed the information. I added, "She had two cell phones, actually. A newer smartphone in a pink cover, and an older flip phone. Because the one she destroyed was the older phone, I had the feeling it wasn't the cell phone she used all the time...maybe it was a backup phone or a burner."

"Burner phone?" Simon said with a short laugh. "Like she's a spy of some sort? That little blond? I've never heard of anything so ridiculous."

"I'm only telling you what I saw."

Pen poised over his notepad, Hopkins asked me exactly what I'd seen. I related the whole incident in detail, then added, "There was something interesting about her calendar, too. I saw it this morning when I was waiting for the interview with you. It may be nothing, but—"

My phone rang again. "Let me put that on silent." I crossed the room. It was another call from Alex. He wouldn't call again unless it was important. "I'm sorry, but I have to take this."

Hopkins waved a hand at me, indicating to answer, and turned to Simon, saying something about an official statement.

"Kate. Where are you?" Alex asked, and I could tell he was walking quickly because of the breathy rhythm of his words.

"In my room."

"Is Holly with you?"

"No. I haven't seen her."

"Good. Steer clear of her. Which room are you in?"

"The Rose bedroom."

Alex repeated this information to someone then a muffled female voice came through the line saying, "This way."

Then Alex was back on the line, his voice strong. "We're almost there."

"We? Where are you?" I asked, but the line was dead.

Before I could call him back, Alex knocked on my open door and stepped inside. Louise followed him in. Today her ponytail and fringe of bangs that framed her round face were tinged purple.

"Alex," I said, crossing to him. "What is going on?"

"I stopped by the pub on the way home and asked Louise about Holly..." He'd been focused on me, but his voice trailed off as he caught sight of Hopkins and Simon.

"This is DCI Hopkins," I said. "And one of the guests, Simon Page," I added. "Simon thinks I jumped to the other balcony, used a hairpin to get the latch open on the glass doors to the Mahogany bedroom, then killed Toby."

Simon lifted his chin. "I saw a piece of evidence and reported it."

"He saw a hairpin on the balcony of the Mahogany bedroom," I said. "I've just told DCI Hopkins that Holly might be a better suspect than me."

Alex gave Simon a long look, then shifted his attention to Hopkins in a way that excluded Simon from the conversation. "Then you'll want to hear this, I think. I pulled up a picture of Holly from Parkview's staff page on the website and showed it to Louise." He motioned to Louise.

She stepped forward. "Louise Clement. I own the White Duck Pub in Nether Woodsmoor. I've lived here most of my life, except for a short stint in Manchester when I was trying out my wings, you might say. Anyway, I recognized Holly's picture as soon as Alex showed it to me. She's older now, and I'll grant you that it's been years since those days when she visited her gran in Aster Cottage, but it's Holly, all right. Same heart-shaped face and freckles. I watched over her a few times for Eileen. I was about, oh I don't know, ten years older than her, I suppose. Amazing to see her grown up now. I'm surprised I haven't seen her in the village with her working here at Parkview."

"You said Aster Cottage was where her grandmother lived?" I asked. "That's in Cottage Lane, isn't it?"

"Yes. Her grandmother lived there until about fifteen years ago, I think. Holly often visited her in the summer. Then Holly's mum died. Tragic situation. Father not on the scene and then the mother, Mary, I think her name was, died from a fast-moving cancer. Holly came here and lived with her grandmother for a bit, then one day Eileen and Holly were gone. I mean, literally overnight. Packed a suitcase of clothes and left. I wondered what had happened to them, sometimes. There were rumors, of course...but no one is sure what happened."

"So Holly lived in Cottage Lane with her grandmother until they moved out suddenly. Could she have been one of the people upset about the changes Beatrice made with the cottages?" I asked.

"No, this was long before that aggro."

I'd lived in Nether Woodsmoor long enough to recognize the shortened term for aggravation, which basically meant trouble.

Hopkins looked up from his notepad. "So you think perhaps the granddaughter, Holly, was the source of the poison pen trouble?"

"It seems possible." I explained about the calendar. "Beatrice said the posts were showing up every three days, and that's what had been ticked off on Holly's calendar. It could be something totally different, but there was also the postcard of Cottage Lane and the picture of the gray-haired woman—probably her grandmother." I frowned. "But isn't it strange that Holly would come to work here and not mention that her grandmother had lived in Aster Cottage?"

"Oh there's more to it than that, luv," Louise said.

Louise had spoken to me, but Hopkins drew her attention to him as he asked, "What do you mean?"

"Just that Eileen was resentful of the Stone family. I don't know all the details because most of it happened before I was born, but I do know that Eileen was engaged to Sir Harold's older brother, but he died before they married. She was bitter about it. It wasn't any secret in the village. My mum said Eileen felt cheated out of her place, that she should be living in Parkview Hall, not in a little cottage in the village."

Louise shook her head, her face creased with disapproval.

"Eileen never liked living in Aster Cottage, which was just plain rude and ungrateful since it was more than generous of Sir Harold's father to let her live there after Cecil died."

"Cecil was the older brother?" Hopkins asked, his pen busy.

"Yes. I don't know exactly when he died, but it was common knowledge in the village that the Stone family let Eileen Brogan live in the cottage. Grace and favor, you know."

Louise saw my frown and said in an aside to me, "Charity. She stayed on there, too, even after she married. Her husband was an engineer. Traveled all over the world, but she had no interest in that sort of life and stayed put. They had a daughter. It's a sad story, all the way around. Her husband died in an accident in one of those foreign places while he was working—was it Egypt? Or perhaps Syria?" Louise shook off the question. "Doesn't matter, I suppose. Eileen stayed on in the cottage, raised their daughter, and then her daughter moved off to London and went to work in one of those big corporations. She married and had Holly."

"I see." So Eileen had lived in the cottage long before the recent controversy about some of the cottages being turned into holiday cottages, which had happened only a few months ago. "But if Holly visited her grandmother, why didn't Beatrice recognize her?" I'd asked Beatrice if any of her employees had links to the village or the cottages, and she'd said they didn't. Beatrice wasn't the type to lie or cover-up. She must not know of Holly's connection to the village and Eileen.

"Eileen didn't want to have anything to do with Beatrice. My mum thinks it was because Beatrice held a role that she would have had, lady of the manor, you know, if things had gone differently."

"She doesn't sound like a pleasant person," I murmured.

"Right cranky, she was. As children, we gave her a wide berth. I was surprised when she asked me to sit with Holly. Holly was a fun child, which made it easy. Good thing, too, because Eileen wasn't exactly generous when it came time to pay me." She shook her head. "That's neither here nor there now. Beatrice wouldn't have seen Holly many times, maybe only two or three times when Holly was a wee one. Holly had darker hair then, too. Light brown, not blond like it is now."

Holly did have dark eyebrows. Maybe she'd dyed her hair blond to disguise herself. "So Holly hasn't come into the pub at all?"

"No," Louise said. "In fact, I don't think I've seen her in the village once."

Hopkins looked back through his notes. "She lives in Upper Benning. Would it be possible for someone to work here at Parkview and not be seen in the village?"

Louise looked perplexed. "I suppose she could do that. The bus does make a stop here, outside the gates. She wouldn't have to get off in the village and change buses. And I suppose she wouldn't *need* to go into the village. We mostly have restaurants and shops. Not much business-related activity. No print shops or anything like that. For that, you have to go to Upper Benning."

I worked out the timeline in my head. "So Eileen lived here in Nether Woodsmoor after her fiancé died until…?"

"It must have been about fifteen years ago, I think. Sir Harold's father had passed. Sir Harold let Eileen stay on in the cottage, which he didn't have to do, you know. It was his father who had let Eileen stay, so after he died, Sir Harold could have asked her to move out, but he didn't."

"I wonder why she moved so suddenly?" I asked.

"She remarried," said a voice from the doorway, and we all turned and saw Beatrice. She'd changed out of her Regency finery and wore her normal attire, a rather boxy white shirt with a mustard-colored skirt and sturdy espadrilles.

"Hello, Louise," Beatrice said and then nodded a greeting to Alex. "Kate, are you okay? Thomas informed me that you'd called for the DCI."

"Yes, but I'm fine…well, except for a few mistaken assumptions." I looked at Simon, who frowned back at me.

"I didn't know that Eileen had remarried," Louise said.

"It wasn't common knowledge," Beatrice said. "Eileen didn't have many close friends in the village. She was glad to cut ties."

"Did you know that Louise thinks Holly is Eileen's granddaughter?"

Beatrice stared at Louise for a second. "Eileen's? I suppose… yes, she would be about the right age. But why wouldn't Holly tell me…" She trailed off, then Beatrice looked to me, clearly caught off guard. "You don't think—Surely, it wasn't her? Did she write those vicious things?"

Hopkins answered. "It is a possibility we will need to investigate."

Beatrice closed her eyes briefly, then nodded. "Holly is in the estate office. I just spoke with her there. You'd better come with me, DCI Hopkins."

"Yes, thank you." Hopkins put his notebook away.

Simon looked at me. "What about her? You're not going to go off and leave her, are you? She could be gone in a moment, off the grounds, and in the wind. Do you have a car?" Simon asked me, his tone suspicious.

"No, I don't. I walked here. I live in Nether Woodsmoor. I'm not leaving Parkview, and even if I did leave, I would only go to my home in the village. I'm not a flight risk."

"What's all this?" Beatrice asked.

"It seems Sir Harold hired Simon to look into the poison pen posts," I began.

"What? Harold wouldn't—" She stopped and frowned at Simon thoughtfully. "Harold did mention something last week. He said he'd taken steps to solve that problem, but we were interrupted, and then in the rush to get ready for this weekend, I forgot to ask him about it, and he…well, you know what he's like," Beatrice said to me then looked at Hopkins. "He tends to become immersed in whatever he's doing to the point that the rest of the world fades away." She looked at Simon. "And you think Holly is the source?"

I said, "No, Simon doesn't seem to have any ideas about the poison pen posts, but he thinks I murdered Toby."

Beatrice turned back to Simon, and he stepped back, holding up his hands. "I can't help what I saw. It was there. I had to report it."

"I don't remember any reporting...only a stun gun."

"Stun gun?" Beatrice said, her voice incredulous.

"Which I have taken custody of," Hopkins said, smoothly inserting himself into the exchange. "I think I can trust Ms. Sharp to give a statement to Constable Albertson?" He looked at me.

"Yes, of course."

"Good." Hopkins removed his phone from his pocket and tapped out a quick text. "I'll have him send for you when he's ready to speak to you. He's set up in the monitoring room." Hopkins turned to Beatrice. "I do need to speak with Ms. Riley."

"Yes, of course. I still can't believe...Eileen's granddaughter, you think?" Beatrice asked Louise.

"Yes. It looks like her."

Beatrice blew out a sigh. "Well, you knew her. I hardly ever saw her."

Thomas came into the room with a man and a woman carrying cameras and large cases.

"My evidence people," Hopkins explained to Beatrice then gave the new arrivals instructions to bag the evidence on the Mahogany bedroom's balcony then dust my balcony for prints.

Beatrice looked concerned until Hopkins said, "Just being thorough, as we must."

She nodded. "Let me take you to the estate office." Simon took a step forward as if to go with them, but Hopkins waved him back with a shake of the head.

Simon didn't look happy. He threw one last frustrated look at me before leaving the room.

The man on the balcony flipped back the case lid and pulled out brushes and powder. Louise, her gaze on him said, "So what's all this about a hairpin?"

I explained about the hairpin in more detail, and Louise sniffed. "That's just silly. That hairpin could have been lying there for weeks. How can they be sure it was yours?"

"Simon said he asked the maid, and there was only one package with the pearls attached."

"But there was another house party before this one. Who's to say that they didn't use another package for those guests?"

"I wish I'd thought to say that."

Louise patted my arm. "Don't worry, luv, all this foolishness will work itself out, I'm sure. But just to make sure, I'll find Ella. She worked the last house party as well. She'll know about the hairpins."

With a last pat on my arm, Louise headed for the door. "Don't wait for me, if you need to get back to the village," she said over her shoulder to Alex. "I'll walk down on my own after I speak to Ella."

"Can you stick around for a while?" I asked Alex. The man was busy dusting powder across the banister. The woman had taken the camera, and I could already hear the click of the shutter through the open balcony doors.

Alex looked concerned. "Sure."

"Good. Where's Grace? Is she here?" I asked, sitting down on one of the floral chairs.

"No, she went back to the cottage." Alex took the other chair. "Twelve is old enough to be on her own for a while."

Because there was a hint of worry in his voice, I said, "Yes, I think she'll be fine. She is probably enjoying being alone. I bet she doesn't get much solitary time at boarding school."

"So this is all because of a hairpin?" Alex asked, his gaze on the man rotating the fluffy brush up and down the balusters.

"Yes, but hopefully, what you and Louise told Hopkins will get him to look for other suspects besides me."

"There's no way he could think you did it," Alex said.

"Unfortunately, it looks like I'm the *only* person who could have done it." I told him about the cameras and the dirt covering the courtyard. "So the balcony is the only way in, and I'm the only one who had access to it."

"Unless someone else got in your room and climbed over the balcony," Alex said slowly. "Just because it's your room doesn't mean you were the one who used the balcony to get to Toby."

"That's true. I hadn't thought of that or of Louise's argument that the hairpin could have been there for ages. I should have had you and Louise here to defend me," I said with a smile.

"Innocent people don't expect to be accused of murder. I'm sure you felt blindsided. No one would think clearly in a moment like that."

A thump sounded from the balcony. The evidence tech flicked the catches on the lid closed and stood. "All finished." He gave a quick nod and went to the other room.

Alex stood. "I should get back to Grace. Come with me?"

"And be considered a fugitive?"

"Only in Simon's eyes. I think Hopkins would understand, especially if you let him know where you'd be."

"No. I'm staying here, at least until I hear what's happened with Holly. If she is related to someone from the village...well, this whole thing might be cleared up in a few hours."

"I knew you'd say that," Alex said. "But I figured it was worth a shot. Call me, let me know what's going on."

"Okay. If you can wait a few minutes, I'll walk to the bridge with you, but first I'd love to change into shorts and a t-shirt."

Alex flared an eyebrow. "Looks as if you might need some help with all those buttons."

"Intriguing thought, but I already have a lady's maid." I motioned Alex to the door as I tugged on the bellpull.

"That's a shame," Alex said with a wicked grin.

SHORTS AND A T-SHIRT felt amazingly light and cool, and the breeze sweeping over my bare arms and legs felt delightful, even slightly risqué, after being swathed head to toe in fabric. The clouds were thickening and now completely covered the sky. The wind had picked up, too, and whipped through the trees.

I'd walked with Alex down to the bridge and said goodbye to him there. He'd gone on to the village, but I paused, elbows resting on the still-warm golden stones of the bridge, watching the water swish and eddy around the bridge supports. The overnight storm must have drenched the whole area upriver because the water was higher than usual. The swirling currents doused the green grass on the banks that was usually above the waterline.

I took a few moments to listen to the sound of the running water and study the busy current. Unlike the section of the river that ran through Nether Woodsmoor, which was wide and smooth, yet fast moving, this portion of the river dropped several feet before and after the bridge as well as curving through the landscape, creating several little bubbling and frothing cataracts. Above the sound of the water, I heard a faint yipping, probably Beatrice's two mop-like dogs. I hadn't seen them since I'd met with Beatrice. They must be confined to the staff areas during the house party.

I reluctantly pushed off and headed back to Parkview, taking the path that wound from the bridge to the front gates. When the golden stone mansion came into view, I cut across the drive and made for the west wing, thinking that since I'd been out of the house, I'd go by the monitoring room and see if Constable

Albertson was ready to take my statement. I could go in the side door near the back of the west wing and spend a little more time outdoors. I headed for the wide gravel avenue lined with hedges on one side and the towering wall of the west wing on the other.

I came around the corner of the house and collided with a woman, jarring her so that her tote bag fell off her shoulder, and its items scattered across the path.

"I'm so sorry. I didn't see you—" I broke off. Two items that had fallen on the path—a postcard of Cottage Lane and a photo of a gray-haired woman—seemed to leap out at me. I picked them up.

"No worries." Holly busily gathered up the other items, several calendar sheets torn from a blotter, a half empty bag of crackers, and a small pot with an African violet, which had spilled dirt onto a pink sweater.

"You're leaving," I said quietly.

CHAPTER 12

"JUST FOR THE DAY," HOLLY said brightly as she pushed the sweater into the tote bag without brushing off the dirt.

We'd both been squatting as we retrieved her things. She snatched up the potted plant, the last item, and stood. She hooked the straps of the bag over her shoulder and held out her hand for the postcard and photo I held. "Thanks so much…"

Her voice trailed off when I didn't hand them over.

"You're leaving permanently," I said.

Her wide open eyes narrowed, and her smile disappeared. "I need those, please."

"So cute, these cottages," I said. "I live in one, did you know that?"

"No. That's interesting." Her tone indicated she couldn't care less. She glanced around. "Look, I do have to go."

While I knew that if I left Parkview, I wasn't going far. I thought the opposite was the case with Holly. Once she cleared those gates, she'd be as far away as possible and probably difficult to find. I scanned the grounds. Nothing to see but a row of hedges and the west wing's wall of windows. No one else was on the path, and the only noises were the distant purr of a car engine and the bark of a small dog.

"Why did you do it? Why did you write those vicious things?"

"I don't know what you're talking about," she said, but her face flushed.

"DCI Hopkins wants to speak to you. He knows about your history, your connection to the village."

Holly looked at me for a long moment, then suddenly lunged forward. She ripped the postcard and photo out of my hand and shoved my shoulder. I stumbled backward, but managed not to fall. Holly sprinted away down the path.

I took off after her, but I'm more of a walker than a jogger. Despite being encumbered with the tote bag, which thumped against her side, she lengthened the distance between us. I was never going to catch her. And if I did, what was I going to do? Tackle her and hold her down?

Holly cleared the end of the path and disappeared around the front of the house. I pounded along behind her, huffing and panting as I reached the end of the path and rounded the corner. Holly, kicking up bits of gravel on the front drive, was making for the long drive to the main gate. Another figure was on the path walking toward Holly. Waverly in all his well-tailored splendor was moving at a dignified pace up the drive toward the house, Beatrice's two little dogs straining at the leashes he held.

I stopped, gathered my breath and put two fingers in my mouth, then let out a piercing whistle. The dogs swiveled their heads toward me. I gulped in more air and whistled again. At the second whistle, the dogs let off a string of yips and lunged in my direction. Caught off-guard, the leashes slipped from Waverly's hand.

The dogs, their ears flopping, little legs churning, and leashes trailing out behind them, headed for me on a diagonal course that took them directly toward Holly. Her gait checked as the dogs beelined toward her. She sidestepped first one way, then the other, finally heading for the edge of the path as she tried to avoid them. The dogs split neatly around her, as if it had been choreographed. The ground along the path was lower, and the dip in elevation must have caught Holly by surprise because she tumbled into the grass.

The dogs reached me, joyfully pawing at my shins. I rubbed their ears. "What good dogs you are. So smart. You knew what to do." I caught their leashes and hurried toward Waverly at a trot. The dogs, game for more running, raced along beside me, their short legs looking as if they were spinning as they covered the ground.

"Don't let her go," I called to Waverly, who was bending over Holly. She held her ankle with both hands and shot me a venomous look as I closed the distance.

"I know you wanted to speak to Ms. Riley, but I'm not sure such extreme measures were needed," Waverly said, impassively.

HOLLY, her rapidly swelling ankle propped on a pillow, lifted her head from the rolled arm of the chesterfield sofa when Beatrice and Sir Harold walked into the library followed by Hopkins. "I'm sorry I didn't let you know in person I was leaving," Holly said to Beatrice.

Waverly had stayed with Holly while I returned to the house and summoned one of the burlier footmen, who had carried Holly back to Parkview and deposited her where Waverly indicated, which was the closest room, the library. I had faded to the side of the room, near the door. No one asked me to leave, and I wanted to make sure Holly didn't convince Beatrice she was only leaving early for the day.

Beatrice waved a square of yellow paper. "Yes, a resignation by sticky note is not good form. Although, I'm not sure, 'Must leave. Sorry,' qualifies as a letter of resignation." I leaned back against the shiny surface of a worktable stacked with oversized books of maps. I should have known Beatrice would be savvy enough to catch onto Holly's subterfuge. Waverly opened the door, balancing an icepack on the silver tray. He took one look around the room and melted back out the door, shutting it noiselessly.

A flush filled Holly's face. "I'm sorry I didn't tell you, but there has been an…an emergency. A family emergency. I have to leave immediately." She struggled upright, swinging her leg off the sofa with a grimace.

Hopkins said, "That won't be possible. I need you to answer some questions."

"I can't. I told you I have to go—"

"Why did you do it, Holly?" Beatrice said, her tone hurt. "Why did you say those horrible things online?"

Holly looked up at Beatrice, and her face transformed from the pitiful expression she had worn. Now her mouth was set and her eyes were hard. "Because under all this…" she gestured around the room, indicating the towering windows with their elegant drapes, the rows of glass-fronted bookcases, the polished tables and plush chairs scattered around the Oriental rugs, the high ceiling with its roundels above the delicate crystals of the chandeliers and said, "…this showy grandness, you're dishonest and low. You put on a good show—all lady of the manor. You come across as someone who cares about the little people, but, all the while, the only thing that matters to you is getting more and more. You don't care who you hurt."

Beatrice looked as if Holly had slapped her across the face. Sir Harold, who had been hovering to the side, moved forward and placed one arm around Beatrice's shoulder, encircling her protectively. "That is enough," he said, in a commanding tone that I'd never heard him use before.

Holly ignored him, her breath quickening, and her face flushing a darker red. "At least you pretend to be nice," she said to

Beatrice. Holly's face contorted as she shifted her angry gaze to Sir Harold. "You don't even go that far. You don't even know or care what is going on, except for one thing...money. Then you're all attention."

Sir Harold stared at Holly a long moment, only his nostrils flared as he breathed deeply. The ticking of an ormolu clock on the mantle sounded in the sudden quiet. I tensed, thinking that Sir Harold was probably one of those people who had a long fuse, but when they became angry, they were spectacularly angry.

Beatrice threw a concerned glance at Sir Harold as she asked Holly, "What *are* you talking about?"

"Sure, he smiles vaguely," Holly spit out, oblivious to—or unconcerned about—the rising anger on Sir Harold's face or the bewilderment on Beatrice's face. "He didn't care when he turned an old lady out of what had been her home for thirty years. No, all that is important to him is the bottom line. Did he care that my gran had to move into a dirty little bedsit after he kicked her out? No, he has no compassion. Everyone should know what kind of hypocrite he is. What kind of hypocrites you both are."

Hopkins opened his mouth, but Beatrice held up her hand. "So you *are* Eileen's granddaughter."

Still breathing raggedly, Holly said proudly, "Yes."

"I can see the resemblance now. I couldn't before." Beatrice's words were tinged with sadness. "But I suppose it was all an act. The helpfulness, the eagerness to learn the job and gain my trust."

The tension eased from Sir Harold's posture. He tilted his head. "Eileen Brogan?" At Holly's nod, Sir Harold continued to stare at her, his face no longer angry. His expression was intense, as if he was trying to classify an unusual butterfly. "You think I turned your grandmother out of Aster Cottage?"

"I *know* you did. That's why I posted those things online," Holly said to Beatrice. "People should know what you're like— what you're both like."

Beatrice reeled back and shook her head, speechless. Sir

Harold removed his arm from her shoulder and took over the conversation, his arms crossed as he leaned toward Holly. "And how do you know this?" He addressed her calmly, almost reminding me of a teacher drawing out a student.

"She told me herself."

"I suppose you wouldn't believe me if I told you that wasn't true?"

"Of course not. In fact, I expected it. That's why I posted things on the Internet. I knew if I confronted you, you'd only deny it."

Sir Harold looked at her a moment more. "Right, then," he said, his tone unruffled. "I suppose the only way to convince you is to show you." He went to one of the bookcases, removed a ring of small keys from his pocket, and unlocked the glass doors that enclosed the books. He ran his finger along a shelf, then switched to the one above it. "Yes, here it is."

He took a book down and flipped through the pages as he slowly walked back across the room. As he passed by me, I saw the book was a ledger filled with neatly handwritten columns. The book fell open. A long piece of paper about two inches wide and eight inches long was pressed into the binding.

He removed the paper and handed the ledger to Holly. "If you'll look at line fifty-seven, I believe, you'll see a payment."

"Eileen Brogan?" Holly's gaze ran along the line to where the amount had been entered. I could see the amount at the end of the line was bigger than most of the other entries and had quite a few zeros after it. Holly gasped at the figure.

"That date is the day before she moved out," Sir Harold said.

Holly stared at the book a moment, then pushed it away. "No, I don't believe you. You took it away, the cottage. You didn't buy it from her."

Sir Harold handed her the piece of paper. I inched closer. When she flipped it over, I realized it was a check, a canceled check with a signature on the back along with the bank stamp.

"But that means…" Holly trailed off, and the check slipped from her hand, floating down to the patterned rug.

Beatrice picked up the check. "It means your grandmother lied to you." She replaced the check in the ledger and closed it then sat down on the sofa beside Holly.

"I don't understand." Holly's voice was small, and her face was perplexed. "I thought Gran didn't own the cottage."

"She didn't," Beatrice said. "Harold's father let her live there after Cecil passed away so unexpectedly. Harold honored the agreement when he inherited. Eileen lived there even after she married and had your mother and later when she was a widow."

"But she told me you forced her out. Made her leave." Holly looked at the ledger. "I don't see how…I mean, she told me…"

Beatrice sighed and looked as if she didn't want to go on. "Eileen met a man…not a gentleman, I'm afraid. But she didn't know that then. None of us did. He seemed prosperous, if a little…slick." Beatrice paused, her fingers tracing along the edge of the ledger. "He proposed. She accepted. They talked of purchasing a flat in London and investments that were poised to triple their return."

Beatrice glanced toward Sir Harold, who had moved around and was leaning on the back of the sofa. "He tried to convince us to invest as well, but Harold wouldn't. Eileen, on the other hand, scraped together everything she had, and then she came to Harold." Beatrice's voice had been reluctant and her gaze tinged with pity as she watched Holly, but now her voice changed. It was charged with indignation. "She demanded Harold pay her for the cottage. She said that Harold's father had intended her to own it, but never done the paperwork, which was not true."

Sir Harold patted Beatrice's shoulder and said mildly, "I could see she was convinced…that she'd worked it around in her mind until she believed that. It would have been a long, messy process involving lawyers and—"

Beatrice cut in. "Harold was generous. He gave her the check and had her sign a paper—the lawyers drew it up—saying she released the cottage to the estate and would not present any further claim or some language to that effect. The lawyers have a copy of it still, I'm sure."

Holly gestured at the ledger. "But if you gave her the money, why would she say those things?"

Beatrice's outrage faded quickly, and her tone was back to pity. "Because the man was a fortune hunter. He took it all, all of Eileen's money, as well as the 'investments' of several other people. He left her penniless. Of course, word got back to us here eventually, and we sent word that Eileen was welcome to return, but she wouldn't hear of it. Too embarrassed, I suppose. I'm afraid in her mind, she must have twisted the story so that she wasn't to blame. It's much easier if you can blame someone else for your mistakes. Unfortunately, the story had to have a villain. It sounds as if she cast Harold."

She threw a sad smile at Sir Harold then returned her attention to Holly. "I'm sorry, my dear, but I'm afraid Eileen has lied to you."

"I can't believe it," Holly said, but her gaze stayed on the ledger.

"You know your grandmother better than I do now, I suppose. I haven't seen her in years, but people's personalities tend not to change drastically. Eileen never accepted that the car wreck that killed Cecil was his fault. He'd been drinking. It was a well-known fact, but she always insisted it was the weather, and the fact that the turn was too sharp where the main road met Westonworth Road."

Holly looked down at the rug. "She is good at revising history and assigning blame to someone else." Her voice was quiet, barely above a whisper. "My not making a good score on my exam wasn't my fault. My tutor hadn't prepared me well enough." She looked up at Beatrice, her dazed expression was replaced with growing dismay. "I believed her about you and Sir Harold, and said those terrible things. I wanted to get back at you. Make you pay for what you'd done to her."

"Is that why you murdered Toby Clay?"

I'd been so swept up in the story that I'd completely forgotten about Hopkins, but now he stepped forward, his face still impassive, but there was a light in his eyes as his gaze bored into Holly. "A murder at Parkview is horrible publicity."

Holly's throat worked as she swallowed. "No. I had nothing to do with that, I swear." She scooted back on the sofa as Hopkins approached, shaking her head from side to side. "I didn't do that. I only wanted to expose Lady Stone and Sir Harold, to show the world what hypocrites they were. I know it looks bad. The timing is terrible—that's why I was leaving. I knew that because of the murder there would be an investigation, that you'd find out what I'd done. I destroyed the phone I used to take the photos that I'd posted online. But I swear it was only the posts and pictures...and the note under the tablecloth at dinner," she added, looking back down at the rug. "I wanted to embarrass them in front of their guests. I figured that would hurt them the most."

Her gaze flickered to Beatrice and Sir Harold. "I'm so, so sorry. If I'd known, I never would have...but murder?" She twisted back toward Hopkins. "No. That wasn't me."

"Where were you last night from eleven until two this morning?"

"At home."

"Can anyone confirm that?"

"Yes," Holly hesitated, then said, "Gran lives with me. She was there." She finished in a rush, "I know you won't take her word for it, but it's true. I was there all night. I swear to it. It's a ground floor flat, you see, with a basement. It flooded last night, as it always does—oh," she said suddenly. Her face brightened. "Tom, you can ask him. He's the building manager. We had to call him. He came first, then sent the plumber," she said with relief.

"And what time was this?"

"I'm not sure, exactly. Late. The plumber didn't arrive until nearly one in the morning. You can check my phone," she said, digging into a pocket. She handed the cell phone with the hot pink cover to Hopkins, and he looked through the call logs.

"The plumber's number is in there. He said to call him if we had more trouble. It's supposed to rain again today—oh, it's already started," she said looking at the windows.

Rain was indeed tapping on the windows and running down the panes in rivulets. I'd been so wrapped up in the drama playing out in front of me that I hadn't even noticed it.

"Oh dear," Beatrice said, "And I'd hoped for a clear afternoon for the guests." She looked toward Sir Harold. "What do you think? Will it clear?"

Harold glanced out the window. He had an uncanny knack for being able to predict whether or not it would rain. I wouldn't have believed it, but had seen him do it before. "She's right. It will last until sunset, I think."

"What a shame. I had planned to give a tour of the gardens this afternoon."

Hopkins gave the phone back to Holly. "I'll need you to make a formal statement, and I also need to speak to your grandmother."

"She's home today. She said she was going to stay in."

Hopkins looked to the door and gave a nod. Cannon stepped forward. I hadn't seen her slip into the room. "DS Cannon will take you home."

Holly nodded, subdued.

The door inched open, and Waverly drifted to my side. "Excuse me, Mrs. Sharp. You have a visitor."

"Me?" I asked. Who would visit me? My two closest friends from the village had already been to Parkview today.

"In the sitting room."

CHAPTER 13

*A*S I LEFT, THE LIBRARY, I nearly ran into Jo. She stepped back quickly from the door. "Is Sir Harold in there?"

"Yes, but he's very busy at the moment," I said.

She nodded and moved away, but only after Waverly came out behind me and closed the door firmly then gave her a long stare. Waverly moved down the hall and opened the door to the sitting room. I didn't see anyone. I was about to turn away when a small voice said, "Over here."

Grace, hair sopping wet and shirt plastered to her shoulders, stood in the far corner of the room near one of the windows. "I didn't want to get the rug wet." She looked down at the floor, where a puddle of water was forming around her feet as water dripped from her long hair and from the hem of her untucked shirt. She shivered and looked at me with a miserable expression.

"Grace, what happened?"

"I didn't think it was going to rain. I mean, the sky wasn't even that dark when I left." With her rain-flattened hair, her face looked more rounded.

"It caught me by surprise, too," I said and some of the tension in her shoulders eased, but then she shivered again.

"I got bored. Alex wasn't back, and I thought I'd walk here to meet him, but then it started to rain—just sprinkles at first. I thought it would quit. I was closer to Parkview than the village so I kept walking. By the time I got to the woods inside the gate, it was pouring. So I came to the door, like Alex and I did earlier, but the butler guy said Alex isn't here..." her voice wavered on the last word.

"Perhaps the young lady would like a towel," Waverly intoned from beside me, making me jump. He held out a tray, which now had a stack of towels on it.

"Yes, of course." I took the towels and crossed the room, shaking out one as I walked. I wrapped it around Grace's shoulders and realized a couple of tears sparkled on her lashes.

"I'm sorry," she whispered. "I didn't mean to make trouble. I should have gone back to the cottage, but it would be a long way in the rain."

"It's fine." I draped another towel over her head and tucked it under her dripping hair. "I think perhaps you should take your shoes off." They were coated in mud and bits of wet grass. "I'm sure Waverly knows someone who can clean them." I looked at him, and he nodded.

Grace worked off her shoes, then stripped off her soaked socks. Waverly held out the silver tray that he had used to deliver the towels. Grace hesitated a moment, then deposited the sodden pile of footwear on the tray with a worried glance at him.

"We'll get you into some warm clothes, and you'll be fine," I said.

"Should I have tea sent up to the Rose bedroom?" Waverly asked.

"Yes, good idea." I was glad to see some of the worry drop off Grace's face. She used the edge of the towel to dab at her saturated bangs and then wiped her eyes. I pretended not to see.

~

ONCE GRACE and I were in my room, I opened the cabinet doors and revealed the tub.

"Brilliant! I want one of these in my room at school." She sounded more like her normal self.

"I'll ask Ella if there might be some clothes you can wear while yours dry, and I'll call Alex."

"Oh, he won't be worried. I left him a note."

"Still, I think I better call."

"I can do it." Grace removed a phone from a pocket on her shorts. "I don't think it got too wet."

"I think the first order of business is to get you warmed up." Grace was only shivering occasionally, but I knew she had to be chilled. "Extra towels are on that shelf there. Add some of that bubble bath, if you want." I tugged on the bellpull then headed for the door.

"Kate," she said, and I paused with my hand on the door. "I know this is a bother. Thanks."

"Anyone could have gotten caught in the rain. It's no big deal."

"That's not what my mom would say. She'd say it *was* a bother. She hates it when I'm a bother. That's why she said boarding school was a good idea."

My hand tightened on the handle. I knew all about mother-daughter conflict, but I had a feeling that Grace had a whole different set of issues to deal with than I did.

At least, my mom *thought* she had my best interests at heart. Granted, my definition of "best interests" and hers were very far apart. She wanted different things for me than I wanted for me. From what I'd heard about Grace's mom, her own interests were her top priority...maybe even her only priority. But perhaps that was unfair. I'd never met the woman, after all. Grace had shown that she could be...challenging, to say the least. On the other hand, she had been near tears in the sitting room, which seemed an extreme reaction to finding yourself stranded in a strange house during a rainstorm, but it was quite a grand house. The setting was intimidating, and if she'd been afraid I would be angry and make her walk back to the village in the driving rain...well, maybe that was the reaction she usually got from her mom.

"No harm done," I said, but Grace still looked worried, so I added, "As Louise would say, 'no worries, luv.'" I said it in my best imitation of Louise's accent, and Grace smiled. "I'll be back soon."

I closed the door behind me as I stepped into the hall where I met Ella. "Did you need something?" she asked.

"Would there be any clothes in the house that would fit a twelve-year-old?" As I explained what had happened, a crack of thunder shook the house, rattling the window panes. Ella glanced up at the ceiling. "The bridge is going to flood, and it will be tomorrow for sure before I can get home."

"It didn't flood last night."

"No, but two storms so close together on top of all the rain we've had this summer," she shook her head. "It will happen. It usually does. I'll see about those clothes. I'm sure I can find something."

I pulled out my phone from my shorts pocket and dialed Alex's number. He sounded hurried and distracted when he answered. "Kate, I can't talk right now. I can't find Grace. She wasn't in the cottage when I got home. I've been down to the pub, but she's not there—"

"She's here, at Parkview," I cut in quickly.

"What? She went out in this storm?"

"No, she said it wasn't raining when she left. She thought she'd meet you on the way back, but didn't see you. Then it began to rain, and she was closer to Parkview than the village, so she came on here. She said she left you a note."

"There wasn't a note. Nothing but an empty house...wait." He grunted. "Here it is, under the kitchen table." He blew out a breath then gave a shaky laugh. "I knew she was probably fine, but I couldn't help but worry…"

"Completely normal reaction," I said.

"All right. Well, I'll be up there to pick her up in a few minutes."

"You'd better wait a bit. She's warming up in a bubble bath in my room right now."

"So, in my limited experience with tween girls, I'll translate that to mean it could be an hour or so before she's ready to go?"

"At least." I spotted Constable Albertson coming down the hall in my direction. "You'd better give us two hours. Ella is finding her dry clothes now."

"Okay, see you soon."

I put my phone away. "Have you come to find me for that formal statement?"

"No, we've put it off until tomorrow." As he spoke, Albertson patted his pockets. "I'm needed at the bridge." He found what he was looking for and took out a waterproof cover, which he expertly pulled over his hat. "It's coming down hard out there. Most likely, we'll have to close the bridge."

I didn't do a lot of driving on the roads around Nether Woodsmoor, but I had enough of a grasp of local geography that I understood what he was saying. "So Parkview will be cut off."

"From the main roads, yes. Of course there are always the footpaths, but to get to or from the village without using the bridge here, you'd have to go about seven miles north before you come to the next footpath bridge, and it usually floods as well. Albertson glanced up and down the hall, his gaze lingering on the crime scene tape the evidence technicians had reapplied after photographing the room earlier.

Albertson took a step closer and lowered his voice. "I feel I know you, Ms. Sharp, and I'm pretty confident that you didn't murder Mr. Clay, but someone here did. If the storm continues, you'll be shut up in here with that person. And I know you're not one to sit back and let things ride, especially after those things that Mr. Page said about you, but in this case, I think it would be best to let it alone."

"But DCI Hopkins is here as well as Detective Sergeant Cannon, right?"

"No, ma'am. They left to take Holly Riley home and interview her grandmother."

"I better call Alex to come pick up Grace right away," I said.

Albertson frowned. "Grace?"

"Alex's sister. She's here."

Albertson nodded. "I see." He moved to put his hat on.

"Wait, Constable Albertson, before you go, Hopkins said you reviewed all the footage from the cameras around the estate. He told us no one crossed the courtyard or was seen in the hallways of Parkview during the night."

"That's right. Very quiet, it was."

"So there's no way Holly could have gotten back inside Parkview last night…if she actually left?"

"Oh, she left all right. The video recorded her walking down the drive to catch the late bus at the gate. She departed after dinner was cleared."

"I suppose that makes sense. If she placed the note under the tablecloth, she'd want to see the reaction to it. I wonder if she watched from the hall or the terrace?"

"I couldn't tell you about that, but I do know she walked down the drive and caught the bus to Upper Benning. Her transportation card was used, and the driver confirmed she got on the bus. He dropped her at her usual stop in Upper Benning." Albertson shook his head. "I don't see why Hopkins had to go over to Upper Benning at this moment. Cursed inconvenient time to get formal statements, if you ask me. I've already contacted the building manager and plumber. They both confirm that Holly was at home. But there you go. Hopkins didn't ask me. The DCI is thorough, I'll give you that."

"So she has an alibi." My heart sank. Since Hopkins had asked Holly where she was between eleven at night and two in the morning, the police must have narrowed the time of death to that window. If Holly was in the clear for those hours, did that mean that Hopkins would be back to looking at me as a worthy suspect again? I didn't want him staring at me with his blank face. Who knew what scenarios he was running in his mind as he contemplated me?

Albertson positioned his hat on his head and gave me a nod. "Stay safe, Ms. Sharp."

I stared at the crime scene tape over the door to the Mahogany bedroom. If Monique was out cold all night and no one crossed the courtyard or came down the hallway, how had Toby been killed? It seemed an impossible puzzle. I ran my gaze along the hallway, searching the corners of the ceiling...well, perhaps there was another way.

CHAPTER 14

"*L*OOK AT THIS MESS." BEATRICE gestured to the files and stacks of papers that tottered on the windowsill. "No thought for order. So inconsiderate. From now on, the DCI can use Holly's old desk."

"I suppose she won't be needing it." I checked my watch. Before I'd left the hallway, I'd tapped on the door to the Rose bedroom and told Grace to finish up her bath, and that I'd be back in a few minutes. On the way downstairs, I'd called Alex and told him that he should come pick up Grace in case the bridge flooded.

Beatrice's hands dropped to her side. "Such a sad situation. As Holly went out the door of the library, she apologized again. She looked as if she did mean it." Beatrice picked up another pile and deposited the tower of papers on one corner of her desk. The pile listed to the side, and I quickly put out a hand and shoved them back into a stack. Beatrice added another stack to the other side of the desk, nodded her head in satisfaction and then dropped into her chair. "Of course, I believed Holly was a happy, trustworthy employee until today. Maybe she's still acting, putting on a show of being contrite." Beatrice swiveled her chair and watched the rain course down the tall windows. "It is a shame. She did her job quite well." Beatrice shook her head and scooted her chair closer to the desk. Her tone was brisk as she asked, "What can I help you with?"

"I had a question about the security of the video cameras."

"It's a top notch system. We didn't skimp on any of that. It was installed a few months ago. Quite expensive, but I think it will be worth it in the end. It does help us monitor what goes on here more easily."

"So could someone outside the system access it?"

Beatrice raised her eyebrows. "To tamper with it?"

"That's what I was wondering, yes."

Beatrice shook her head. "Not likely. We've put all the security precautions in place—we password protect the cameras and change the passwords frequently. Even the door to the monitoring room has a keypad lock that's changed every two or three days. It records each time someone enters and exits. Every person who has access to the room has a different code so we can track who has been in and out of the room, and only four of us have access—me, the head of security, his assistant, and Sir Harold. I pulled the records myself for the DCI. No one unauthorized has entered. Of course, no system is fool-proof, but the DCI," Beatrice threw a dark look at her desk—it seemed as if Hopkins would get an earful when he returned—"had his team look at it. They said it was secure."

I sat back with a sigh.

"You're disappointed," Beatrice said, watching my face. "You thought someone had manipulated the recordings or disabled a camera to get into the Mahogany bedroom unseen."

"I'd thought it might be a way."

Beatrice shook her head "I'm no expert, and I'm sure there are ways around most security systems, but the DCI's people seemed satisfied that no one had tampered with our set up."

A gust of wind dashed a cascade of rain at the windows.

Lightning flashed, brightening the room for a second. "I'd better get back to my room and see if Grace is ready to go."

"Grace?"

"She was caught in the storm and made her way here. She's having a hot bath while Ella finds her dry clothes."

"There's no need for her to leave. She can stay for dinner, if you think she'd like that sort of thing. Or you can have a tray sent up to her." Beatrice glanced out the window. The afternoon had turned gloomy and overcast when the rain started, but now the sky was much darker. It looked like it was nearer twilight rather than mid-afternoon.

"I'm sure it would be a unique experience for her, but Constable Albertson says the bridge may flood, and I've called Alex to come pick her up."

Beatrice stood and walked to the windows. Hands on hips, she surveyed the scene. "Yes, the footpath to the gardens is flooding, and I can see pools forming on the low lawn. If we see that, we know we'll be cut off for a couple of hours, perhaps a day. So, yes, getting her back to the village is probably the best idea."

"In that case, I better get moving."

As I walked along the west wing on my way back to the main entrance of the house, my steps slowed as I reached the monitoring room with its glowing keypad on the handle. A man in a navy blazer sat in front of the constantly changing images on the monitors. It certainly looked secure, and Hopkin's team hadn't found anything suspicious about it, so I would have to assume the security footage was accurate...as much as I would like to assume the opposite. A disabled camera or missing footage would go a long way to explain how someone had gotten into the Mahogany bedroom.

I picked up my pace again and reached the black and white marble of the entry hall where I heard Monique's voice. "Are you sure?"

I paused and spotted her holding a phone to her ear with one hand, the other propped on her hip. She stood on the landing where the stairs branched to the different sides of the gallery that overlooked the entry. She faced the window, but it didn't look as if she were taking in the view of the rain pounding down outside.

I slowed my steps. I wanted to give her a wide berth. She wore a black short-sleeved sweater with gray herringbone pants and three-inch red Louboutin pumps. Her hair curls, which had been so flattened and disarranged this morning, now flawlessly framed her face. She had on fresh makeup...eyeliner, mascara, and a layer of red lipstick.

"And the p and e?" she asked, her voice clipped. She listened then said, "Fine. Buy seven hundred shares. Text me when the transaction goes through." She paced a few steps away, ran her finger down the nose of a Roman bust situated in the corner of the landing, then turned and strode back to the window. "And the contract for the perfume deal?...Then keep pushing. I want that wrapped up before the news about Toby breaks...for the publicity, darling. Every news story should have my name and the phrase, 'who has just agreed to distribute her new signature fragrance exclusively through the Saxon and Trilby stores.'"

She turned away from the window and climbed the stairs that went to the gallery on the east side of the house. "I don't see how I'll be able to get away today with all this rain. Plan on at least tomorrow afternoon. Let's hope the police stop being so tiresome. Imagine telling me I can't have my own belongings. It's absurd. Find out who is in charge of this investigation—no, not Hopkins. Find his boss, and get him on the phone, then conference me in. I'll be waiting."

Her voice faded, and I walked slowly up the steps. I had thought Monique was basically a spoiled brat, only interested in clothes, makeup, hair, and which trendy restaurant everyone was eating at now, but she'd actually sounded rather knowledgeable on the phone. Very business savvy, and, as unsavory and almost mercenary as her publicity plan was, it would get the news about her new fragrance line out there.

I tapped on the door of my room, then stuck my head around it. "Are you a prune yet?"

Grace was wrapped in a fluffy white robe. She examined the fingertips of one hand critically. "Yep, wrinkled, but warm."

"Good." I stepped into the room. "Any sign of clothes?"

Ella was right behind me. "Here you are. Shirt, jeans, socks. I couldn't find any shoes, but Waverly says Miss Grace's shoes should be here in a moment.

"Great. I'll leave you to change. Alex is on the way."

Ella cleared her throat. "I thought you'd want to know that one of the groundskeepers came up to the house and says the bridge to the village is under water. No one will be able to cross."

CHAPTER 15

"WE'RE ALL STUCK IN A big country house in a rainstorm?" Grace said. "Smashing."

My phone rang. It was Alex. I tucked the phone under my chin and took the clothes from Ella as I answered.

"The bridge to Parkview is closed," Alex said as I handed the clothes to Grace, and Ella exited the room. Alex's voice continued, the line resounding with the crackle of static that coincided with a burst of lightning that flashed at the windows, "They're turning everyone back. I can't get there."

"We just heard."

"Is Grace worried? Scared to be stuck there after a murder?"

"No, she's taking it quite well. In fact, I'd say she is a bit excited."

Alex's voice relaxed. "Ghoulish little thing. Put her on, will you?"

I handed the phone over. Grace's side of the conversation consisted of murmuring *yes* several times. I went to one of the sets of glass doors, flicked the hook out of the latch, and stepped onto the balcony. The sound of pounding rain drowned out Grace's words. The shelter of the roof overhang covered the balcony, but water poured down from the edge of the roof, clearing the edge of the balcony and dropping straight to the flagstones of the courtyard below where it churned and gurgled then pooled around several drains. The sheer amount of water spilling from the clouds had overwhelmed the drainage system, and puddles of water were inching wider and wider from the drains. The broken planter had been repaired and only water covered the flagstones.

Some raindrops splashed onto the balcony's railing and mixed with the remnants of the fingerprint powder. I looked at the Mahogany bedroom's balcony. It was in the same soggy state as mine with a thin layer of water that had ricocheted off the various surfaces, landing on the balcony floor. The hairpin was gone. I shook my head. If Simon hadn't spotted that hairpin earlier today, it might have been swept off the balcony in the overflow of the rain, and I wouldn't be worried about my next conversation with Hopkins.

I was staring at the Mahogany bedroom's balcony, thinking more about the situation than looking at the balcony when an oddity in the coloring of the balusters caught my eye. The last baluster, the one closest to the house, had a horizontal stripe that looked as if it had been scrubbed clean. I leaned closer. The area, about an inch wide, was near the base of the baluster, and was lighter than the rest of the stone. I stepped back and looked at the rest of the balusters, but none of the others had a lighter stripe.

I frowned, trying to figure out what could have made that mark. Had someone been able to get a rope around the baluster and climb up from the courtyard? But that was impossible because the courtyard had been covered with unmarred mud. There had been no footprints. And, even if that were the case, wouldn't the mark where the rope had rubbed be at the base of the baluster rather than a couple of inches above it?

"Odd." I turned and scanned the balusters that edged my balcony for similar marks. There weren't any. I peered across the way to the rooms on the east wing. Maybe someone staying over there had seen something...noticed something?

"What's odd?"

I didn't realize I had spoken aloud. I turned and found Grace leaning out the balcony doors, now dressed in the clothes that Ella had provided, which were a bit saggy.

"Oh, nothing. Just trying to figure out something."

"Who killed Toby Clay?"

"Er—no, of course not."

Grace just looked at me. "Really, Kate? You expect me to believe that you're not interested in finding out who did it?" She did scathing skepticism as only a pre-teen can. I was glad she had recovered from her teary uncertainty in the sitting room, but I wasn't sure I wanted her to go all the way back to the other end of the scale to snarky tween.

"I know about those other times that you helped the police. Alex told me," Grace said.

"Okay, yes. To be perfectly honest, I was trying to figure out how someone got into the room."

"The locked room," Grace said.

"How do you know about that?" I asked.

"Everyone was talking about it at the pub. How no one could have come up from the courtyard because there were no footprints in the dirt and how the halls and roof are monitored. Some people think it was the ghost."

"The ghost?"

"Yes, the Lonely Lady. Parkview Hall is haunted, didn't you know?"

"Every stately home needs a ghost. Part of the package, I suppose."

"Yes," Grace agreed. "This one is a daughter of one of the baronets from ages and ages ago—I don't remember which one. Her family wouldn't let her marry the man she loved. She drowned herself in the river."

"So she takes her revenge on a visiting houseguest hundreds of years later?" I asked.

Grace shrugged. "I didn't say *I* believed it. Ghosts don't murder people. Anyway, back to the locked room thing..."

I pressed my lips together for a moment. She was here, and she knew all about the crime and the locked room. It was no use pretending that it wasn't interesting to me as well. "That's the key, I think. Once the police figure that out, they'll know who the murderer is."

"Right. The police." The sarcasm was back.

"It does...interest me, in a very personal way, in fact. But I have to watch out for you. Your brother would kill me, if something happened to you."

"Then we'll just concentrate on the puzzle about the room."

"Grace—"

"What else are we going to do? We can't leave. We're stuck here. We can't go outside. I saw the schedule of optional activities on your dressing table." She looked at her watch. "The hands-on *Needlecraft in the Regency* lesson starts in fifteen minutes, but I don't want to spend my time learning to sew. I already tried at school, and I know I'm terrible at it. I bet you don't want to go either."

"All the other activities were outdoors," I said, thinking of the schedule. It had been on the tray this morning when Ella brought my breakfast.

"So they will be canceled. We might as well sleuth a little... subtly, you know."

I looked at Grace with her eager face and her dark eyes, which were so like Alex's. At least she wasn't sullen and scared. And I had a feeling that no matter what I said, she was determined to look for clues. Better to stay with her and keep an eye on her than have her sneaking off on her own. We did have several long hours to fill before dinner. "I suppose it couldn't hurt to do some research on the other guests. Maybe ask a few questions. *Maybe*," I emphasized.

Grace smiled widely. "Great. So where do we start?" Without waiting for an answer she said, "We should question the suspects. That's always what Poirot and Miss Marple do."

"I think we should start slowly." I picked up the welcome packet from the nightstand. "Let's read everyone's bio and see if anything stands out." Simon had been hiding behind a fake identity and Holly had hidden her background. Maybe someone else was putting up a front.

Clearly Grace wasn't as excited about reading as she was about grilling suspects, but she took the section of papers I handed her and settled down on the floor, legs crossed. She fanned the pages on the rug.

"You can have the other chair." I sat down by the fireplace.

"I always do my schoolwork like this," she said, her eyelids flickering as she scanned the lines on the pages. "I like the floor. I'm starting with the dead guy. The books always say if you understand why the victim was killed then you'll know who the murderer is."

"That's probably true, but Toby was a high-powered businessman. He probably had lots of enemies." I didn't quite believe Monique's assertion that no one disliked Toby enough to kill him.

"Well, then someone who had a connection to him," Grace said.

I turned my attention to the first bio, Monique Clay. As his wife, she certainly had a connection to Toby. I had to admit that Grace was right. Except for Monique, none of the other guests had an obvious connection to Toby. Why would someone kill him? And why kill him here at Parkview? And how did the person get into the room?

I shook off my wandering thoughts and focused on the bio of Monique. What little I knew about her came from the headlines of grocery store tabloids. Her family ran an international pharmaceutical business, and Monique had spent her late teen years jetting from one exotic destination to another, the tabloids snapping pictures of her bad behavior. A totaled car on the roads of Monaco and an arrest for driving under the influence in Hollywood were the most notable events. Then she and Toby had a whirlwind romance, which meant more tabloid fodder, especially since she was cast in the role of the "other woman" who had broken up Toby's decade old marriage.

Where was Toby's ex-wife? I reached for a pen and made a note in the margin. If anyone had motive, it was surely her.

Monique's bio in the packet didn't mention any of those topics in the tabloids, only that she and Toby lived in London, and that she was "the host of the popular chat show *Fashionista*." It looked as if she'd thought of the request for a bio as another publicity opportunity.

"I didn't know Monique was on a chat show," I said.

Grace looked up. "She was, but it was canceled."

"Did you watch it?" I asked, curious.

"Yeah, I watched the first episode online with some of the girls at school, but it was boring."

I pulled my laptop toward me and searched for the show's name. The most recent news stories announced that Monique's venture into entertainment media had bombed. "Can this stilted and perfectly coiffed mannequin be the train wreck we all love to hate?" asked one reviewer. "Skip it," was the verdict of another, saying the show should be called *What Not To Watch*.

I shook my head. Monique certainly wasn't my favorite person at the house party, but surely reviewers didn't have to be so snarky and cruel.

An article further down the list, an entertainment industry source, had the headline, "Monique's Bottom Line Feels The Hit as *Fashionista* Bombs." I clicked on it and read that Monique had created her own production company to produce the show.

"Rumors are circulating," the article concluded, "that business-savvy husband Toby has pulled his financial support from the venture but says to be on the lookout for Monique's next project."

I wondered if that next project was her signature fragrance. I switched to the next bio, Simon Page.

I skimmed the page, but the details were extremely brief and most of it, I now knew, was fabricated. I went on to Jo and Jay Funderburg. They lived in Miami. Jo listed travel as her favorite hobby, while Jay had put down baseball, which certainly held true with what I'd seen of him during the weekend. I frowned at Jo's name, remembering last night before dinner when she asked to speak to Sir Harold alone. And she had hovered outside the library today and asked for him. Maybe the discovery of Toby's body had caused their meeting to be postponed, and she was hoping to talk to him this afternoon? Why did she want to talk to Sir Harold privately anyway?

Even though Holly had an alibi, there was still the question of whether or not the murderer had intended to kill Sir Harold. Of all the guests, Jo had sought out Sir Harold more frequently than anyone else, even more than Michael, who shared his interest in butterflies. You'd think a researcher with access to the owner of one of the premier collections of butterflies in Britain would have a few more questions for Sir Harold.

"You have the bio for Michael?" I asked Grace after flipping through my remaining pages.

"Michael Jaffery? Yes, right here."

"What does it say?"

She skimmed the text. "Not much. Basically just that he's from Essex and is writing a book."

"Hmm."

"Hmm. What?"

"I don't know. He takes a lot of photos, but not of butterflies."

Grace said, "Maybe he likes photography, too?"

"Possibly, but he takes the photos on his phone and says they are for his mom."

Grace moved his sheet to a different pile. "He goes into the suspicious pile."

"Okay, anyone else in that pile?"

"No," Grace said with a sigh. "Everyone else is completely ordinary-sounding. Amanda is a chef—I wish we could try some of her desserts, they sound absolutely brill—at a hotel in London. Beth's bio is all about her wedding. I don't think she works. It doesn't say."

"Her wedding is pretty much all she talks about."

"And Torrie works at a community center and likes to run marathons." She tapped her phone. "I checked all the names online and didn't see anything unusual."

"That's a good idea." I typed Jo's name into the search engine on my laptop. The list of results included several images of people, one of which was Jo. I clicked on the image.

"What about you?" Grace asked. "Anyone suspicious?"

"Nothing concrete—" I broke off and looked closer at the webpage, which was a list of employees at Consortium Hotels Group, an exclusive hotel chain. The smiling dark-haired woman was Jo, but her name was listed as Jo Atal, not Jo Funderburg. And her title was Chief of Global Development.

CHAPTER 16

"*S*HE'S GOING IN THE SUSPICIOUS pile." Grace peered over my shoulder at the laptop. "That's not the name on her bio."

"No, it's not, but sometimes women use a different name in business. It might be her maiden name, and she simply kept using it for business after she married," I said, but my thoughts were racing. Toby's business had branched out from online gambling into many other areas. Was he involved in the hospitality business? Were he and Jo competitors? Would his death benefit Jo in some way?

"Still...it's something that stands out," Grace said. "You said that's what we were looking for."

"I did." I handed her the paper, and she stacked it on the one with Michael's name.

"Anyone else?"

I glanced back through the bios, and fingered Monique's paper. It sounded as though Monique was better off with Toby alive, if he'd been supporting her business ventures. I wondered what would happen now that he was dead. How was his company structured? Did he have a board of directors who would take over the management? They might be a lot less financially supportive of Monique's business ideas.

I flipped to the next page, which was Audrey's bio. I didn't know enough about her to make a decision on whether or not she had any motive to kill Toby or even any connection to him. She seemed to be genuinely interested in reenacting a Regency house party. I pondered for a moment, trying to picture her sneaking—somehow—into the Mahogany bedroom and killing Toby. Nope, I just couldn't see it. I didn't think she was anything other than what she appeared to be. Besides, where would she get all those gorgeous historically accurate dresses that fit her exactly, if she wasn't a true Janeite and Regency fan girl?

I felt the same way about Jay, and a quick Internet search backed up his claim that he worked in Internet technology as a computer programmer. His Facebook page showed that his interest in baseball wasn't feigned.

"Nope, I think that's all."

"So what should we do next? Search the room next door?"

"No. There will be no breaking and entering. The room is sealed with police tape."

"No, it's not."

"It's not?"

"No, Ella brought my shoes back while you were on the phone, and she told me that her next job was to clear it out. She looked a little spooked actually."

"Did she?" I headed for the door.

The crime scene tape was gone, and the door to the Mahogany bedroom was propped open. A rolling cart with cleaning supplies and stacks of towels was parked beside the open door. Ella came out of the door, a trashcan in one hand and a mop in the other. "Oh, Kate." She stopped short. "I mean Miss Sharp." She bobbed a curtsey, quickly shifting into her role.

"What's happening? I thought this room was closed."

Ella glanced quickly up and down the hallway. "It was. We had orders not to go near it, but then a little while ago Mrs. King told me the police had given permission for Mrs. Clay's things to be removed and the room to be cleaned." She lowered her voice. "I think Mrs. Clay pulled some strings to get all her clothes and stuff back. Her clothes are extremely important to her."

"I guess Monique got through to the head honcho then."

Ella frowned. "I don't understand."

I waved a hand. "Not important. And I'm keeping you from your work. Go ahead."

Ella slid the mop into a holder on the side of the cart, then dumped the contents of the trashcan into a larger bag attached to the cart.

"I'm surprised the police didn't take that," I said, nodding to the cascade of makeup smeared tissues, a couple of gum wrappers, an empty mint box, and the welcome packet with the guest bios as they fell into the trash container on the cleaning cart.

"They must not have thought it was important." Ella shrugged. "They took practically everything else. Towels, sheets, even some pillows. None of Mrs. Clay's clothes, though, thank goodness."

I nodded. I would hate to think what sort of scene Monique would make if some poor policeman decided one of Monique's designer items should go in an evidence bag.

Grace, who had been hovering at the edge of the door asked, "Can I look around?" In an undertone, she said to me, "To examine the crime scene."

Ella glanced at me. "I suppose it would be okay. I mean, I'm in here, and they didn't say no one else could come in."

"We'll be quick." Grace darted around the cart.

I didn't want to admit it to Grace, but I did want to see the room again. The bed had been stripped of sheets, and the doors of the tall mahogany wardrobe that stood on one side of the room gaped open, the interior empty.

Grace wandered around the room. I was glad to see her hands

were shoved into her pockets. The scents of furniture polish and cleaning fluids filled the room. Every surface had been wiped clean and rubbed until it reflected what little light filtered in on the dim afternoon. The room had a connected bath. I peeked in and surveyed the clean counters and sparkling tile—Ella had done a good job.

When I returned to the room, Grace was walking around the perimeter, tapping the walls with a knuckle. "Searching for a hidden door?"

"Or compartment. Someone could hide in there until after the body was discovered then blend in with everyone."

"I suppose that might have been possible," I allowed, thinking of the chaotic scene when all the guests had pushed into the room. "Find anything?"

"No. And I checked the wardrobe, too. No false back."

"So that eliminates the possibility of Narnia, as well."

"You're laughing at me."

"No, I'm not. It was a good idea, but I think if there was another way into the room the police would have noticed." I moved to the glass doors to the balcony, the one that was closest to my balcony, and examined the small hook and eye that held it closed. I noticed there was a tiny gap between the two doors. I supposed it would be possible to work a hairpin into the gap and force the hook out of its metal ring.

I turned and scanned the room. The only personal thing left was a paperback on the nightstand on Monique's side of the bed. I was surprised to see the title was *Lady Chatterley's Lover*. I opened the cover. Monique's name, written in script that resembled bubbles, was on the inside cover, and there was a bookmark about halfway through the pages. It seemed an odd reading choice for Monique. The latest unapologetically trashy beach read would have seemed more her style, but then again, I hadn't expected her to talk about buying stock so knowledgeably either.

"There's not one single thing here," Grace said, disappointment in her voice as she gazed around the room.

"Come on, we should go. We don't want to get Ella in trouble."

Thunder rumbled as we walked down the hall. "Okay. Where to?" Grace asked. "We could question that Jo lady with the different last names."

I gave her a warning look. "Don't mention that to anyone. If Jo," I paused, considering how to phrase my words, "did have something to do with Toby's death, and she knows you've figured out that she's not who she says she is…"

Grace swallowed. "Right. Not a smart thing to blab about. I won't say anything else."

"Good," I said, but inside I was conflicted. What if we had uncovered a vital piece of information that endangered Grace just because she knew it? The police wouldn't be able to return to Parkview until the storm broke and the river went down, which could be later tonight or even tomorrow.

"Don't look so worried," Grace said. "I can keep a secret. Truly, I can. I went all term without telling—" she stopped abruptly. "See, I can keep a secret."

"Good," I said, but I still felt uneasy.

"So where to?"

"I think we should pay a visit to the east wing and talk to the bridal party."

Grace frowned and lowered her voice. "But none of them are in the suspicious category."

"No, but they might have seen something."

CHAPTER 17

$\mathcal{I}$ TAPPED ON THE DOOR of the Versailles bedroom in the east wing, where Beth, Amanda, and Torrie shared a room.

"It's open, Torrie," called out a voice, which I recognized as Amanda's.

I opened the door an inch. "It's not Torrie. It's Kate. May I come in?"

Amanda looked up from a cardboard box that was open on the bed in front of her, a startled expression on her face. "Ah —sure."

"Sorry to bother you. I just have a quick question... " My words trailed off as I stepped inside the doors, and the grandeur of the room overpowered me. Gilt-bordered mirrors covered every inch of wall space in the huge room, reflecting the crystal chandeliers and the long windows that overlooked the rain-drenched courtyard. Despite the gloomy day, the room was bright. Moving from the hallway to the room, felt like moving from a tunnel into daylight. I'd heard about the Versailles bedroom, but never seen it. It was too unique for any of the filming we'd done for the Jane Austen documentary, and the lighting with all the mirrors would have been a nightmare, but it was incredible.

"Whoa," muttered Grace at my elbow.

"Overpowering, isn't it?" Amanda asked. She shoved a cream-colored belt into a cardboard box. "There. All cleaned up." She came across the room to us, her heels clicking on the parquet floor. "Come in and admire. It still amazes me when I walk in. Down here is the best place to see the whole thing." She pointed to the far end of the room. Three beds along with several other pieces of furniture ranged around the room, but it was so large, the space didn't feel crowded.

"Beatrice told us it was renovated over two hundred years ago. The mirrors and all the swanky stuff were added after one of the old baronets visited Versailles and saw the Hall of Mirrors."

"Just had to have one of his own," I said with a grin.

"Something like that. It's a shame the tour was canceled. Beatrice said she had some other great stories about the room, but was saving them for the tour. Maybe she'll do it tomorrow before we have to leave."

Torrie came in the door, carrying an insulated carafe and a plate stacked with delicate cakes and sandwiches. "Score!" She held up the plate. "High tea for everyone. Hi, Kate. Want to join us...or me, actually. Beth is at the spa, probably having her body wrapped in some horrible smelling goo, and Amanda's job has made her immune to sweets."

"It's sad, but true," Amanda said. "Dessert completely loses its appeal when it's your job."

"I think it looks scrumptious," Grace said.

"This is Grace," I said. "She's staying here until the rain stops."

"Come on over, Grace." Torrie put the plate on a little table by the windows, then turned over a couple of teacups that were already laid out. "We'll have a rainy day tea party. Want some, Kate?"

"Perhaps just a little one." It had been a long time since lunch and dinner was several hours away. I selected a triangular sandwich. Grace went for several of the cakes.

Amanda poured tea for herself. "You said something about a question, Kate?"

"Yes. I was wondering about last night. Did you hear or see anything in the west wing?" I waved at the two pairs of tall glass doors that opened onto the balcony. "Since you're directly across from the Mahogany bedroom, I thought you might have noticed something."

Torrie stirred her tea. "Not me. I slept so hard. It must be all this fresh air—and that run. The combination did me in. And Beth said she slept all night. She's a bit of a night owl, but she turned in when I did. She didn't say anything about noticing lights or movement in the other wing. Of course, anything beyond wedding veils and table decorations for the wedding breakfast are pretty much nonexistent for her right now," she said with a shake of her head. "What about you, Amanda? You stayed up later."

"Yes, I read for a bit, but the curtains were closed," she said tilting her head, indicating the heavy brocade panels.

I moved to the window, my gaze running over the balcony then across the stretch of the courtyard to the other wing. The lights in the Rose bedroom glowed faintly. A movement in the room on the other side of the Rose bedroom, the last room in the wing, caught my attention. I stepped closer and saw it was Monique, pacing back and forth. Her hand was angled up to her head, and although I couldn't see it, I assumed she was talking on her cell phone. With the police locking down the Mahogany bedroom, she would need another room. I watched her for a moment, then looked back at the balcony, stepping closer to the window.

"Do you mind if I go outside for a moment?" I asked.

"Go ahead." Torrie offered the plate to Grace again, and I

thought we better not stay much longer or Grace would spoil her dinner.

I unhooked the little latch and stepped outside. The rain seemed to have let up a bit. The roar of it coming down wasn't quite as loud, but it still fell in a steady cascade, sheeting down from the overhang that protected the balcony.

I stepped carefully over the thin layer of water on the balcony to the corner. Like all the other balconies, this one had two potted boxwoods positioned on each side of the balcony. A lighter strip ringed one of these balusters, too. It looked exactly like the one on the balcony of the Mahogany bedroom. About an inch and a half of the stone looked as if it had been scrubbed or wiped, but on this balcony, the baluster with the unusual marking was not near the back of the balcony like the one on the Mahogany bedroom balcony, but near the front. Maybe it was some sort of flaw or natural striation in the stone? I turned around, examining the rest of the stone balusters, but none of them had a similar mark.

Amanda stepped onto the balcony, her teacup and saucer in one hand. "Find anything?"

"No," I said slowly. "Not really." Not anything I could take to the police.

"Sorry we're not more helpful." She glanced back inside at Grace then lowered her voice. "I can understand why you'd ask. I heard that Simon put the police on to you. That's just low. And absurd. You didn't even know Toby."

"Thanks for the vote of confidence. Simon thought he was being helpful, I suppose," I said, putting it in the best light possible. I still had dinner this evening to get through, and I didn't want us dividing up into tribes or camps like reality show contestants.

I looked around the balcony one last time. "It is a shame that none of you heard anything. I'd half-hoped that there would be something, even a small thing. Anything that might help the police. At this point, it seems the person who got into the Mahogany bedroom must have either conjured themselves into the room or levitated onto the balcony."

As I said the word conjured, a thought drifted into my mind... an association, but the sound of china clattering interrupted my thoughts, and I looked around to see Amanda righting her teacup. "I lost my grip on the handle. Good thing it didn't break. So clumsy. It's getting to be a habit with me. Let's get inside."

I followed her back into the room. Grace was dusting crumbs from her fingers. I thanked them for talking to us, and Grace nicely added her thanks for the tea, and we left, but the whole time I was trying to reach back to the thought that had flitted in and out of my mind so quickly.

Conjuring...that was it. Something had popped into my mind, something associated with the word...Sleight of hand or illusion... Grace's voice penetrated my thoughts. I caught the word *slacklining* and realized she was back on that subject.

"...so anyway, that would be so much fun, don't you think?"

I blinked and looked at Grace. "Slacklining? I don't think Alex wants you doing that. Besides, it's pouring outside." We came to the gallery, and I saw Waverly moving at his sedate pace across the checkered tile of the entry hall below us.

And then I had it. As we moved down the grand staircase, I realized it was Waverly and his juggling and plate spinning that had come to mind when I thought of conjuring. Thomas had said Waverly had been in the circus and had performed as a magician. If anyone would know about sleight of hand and appearing and disappearing from locked rooms, it would be a magician, wouldn't it?

CHAPTER 18

"*H*URRY," I SAID TO GRACE, whose face had closed down when I mentioned that slacklining was still off the table. "I need to catch Waverly."

"Who's Waverly?"

"The butler."

"You think the butler did it?" Grace whispered as we motored down the first set of stairs.

"No idea. It would be rather clichéd, I know." I had pored over those bios of the guests, but completely ignored the staff even though they had been in the house, too, and had just as much opportunity as anyone else to get into the Mahogany bedroom. How many servants were there in Parkview? My heart sunk at the thought. Too many for me to make much headway, I was sure.

But I could start with Waverly.

We came to the landing and turned back to the entry, trotting down the last set of stairs. Waverly disappeared through a door on the far right-hand side of the room. We were half-way across the entry when I heard Jo's voice coming from the library. "... sorry to intrude, but I *must* speak to you. It will only take a few minutes. If I could just have a minute alone with you, I think you'll find it worth your while."

My steps checked as we came even with the library door. Jo's back was to me, but I recognized her smooth voice and her glossy black hair, which was twisted up into a chignon. She stood at one end of the worktable, where Sir Harold and Michael were seated side by side.

The worktable was strewn with open books, papers, and at Michael's elbow, a laptop computer. I inched into the doorway and saw the books were open to gorgeous full-color illustrations of butterflies. A tall glass domed display case sat on the table between them. It was filled with several butterflies, but the most eye-catching one was a large one in the center with iridescent blue wings.

Sir Harold stood and blinked at Jo, clearly coming out of the world of butterflies. "Yes, of course. Happy to speak to you."

I had moved into the room enough that I could see Jo's profile. She smiled apologetically at Michael as she said to Sir Harold, "Somewhere private. It is a delicate matter."

"I can leave—" Michael half stood, but Sir Harold waved him back into his chair.

"My office is this way." He stepped out from behind the table and moved to a door at the far end of the room.

Alarm bells went off in my head. The question about the intended victim hadn't been cleared up. If Sir Harold had been the target...no, I couldn't let him go off alone with a woman whose name might or might not be fake. And she had lied—or at least had led everyone to believe she had a much lower profile job than she did. That was two deceptions—that I knew of. There could be more.

"I don't think that's a good idea," I said.

Sir Harold half turned and looked at me over his shoulder. "Ah, Kate."

"Why not?" Jo smiled, but her words had an edge to them, and

I could suddenly picture her in an executive role. "It will only be a moment."

"I'll—ah," Michael stood, looking uncomfortably from Jo to me. "I'll just—umm—make a phone call." He walked quickly out the door, shifting around Grace who had stopped on the threshold. She watched Michael leave then edged farther into the room.

I turned my attention back to Sir Harold. I blew out a deep breath, then said, "I don't think you should meet with her because I'm not entirely sure who she is. Her bio says her name is Jo Funderburg, but her picture is on Consortium Hotels Group's website with her name listed as Jo Atal."

Sir Harold's eyebrows drew together as he muttered the name under his breath.

Jo closed her eyes and gave a tiny shake of her head. "I told my assistant to take care of that," she said in a clipped tone.

Sir Harold's face cleared, and he looked at Jo. "Jo Atal. *You* are Jo Atal? You've been emailing me, but your first name had the letter 'e' on the end of it."

She drew in a breath and put the smile back on her face. Tilting her head slightly, in what might have seemed to be a conciliatory way, at least on the surface, she nodded. "Yes. I'm Jo. And Joe, with an 'e.' I've found that people take me more seriously if they think I'm a man."

She turned toward me. "I can see there has been a misunderstanding, which considering the atmosphere and the events of the last day, is not surprising. You know me as Jo Funderburg, which is my married name. Jay is my husband. Atal is my maiden name. I'd used it for years, and it seemed smarter to keep using it after we married."

She swung back to Sir Harold. "But I assure you, while my name may be a bit confusing—even misleading—I am who I say I am."

"Which is it, then," I asked. "A minor cog in the hospitality industry, which is what you led me to believe and what your bio in the welcome packet says, or are you the Chief of Global Development?"

She sent me a look that I'm sure she used to reign in her assistant, but—thankfully—I didn't work for her. I'd brushed up against some pretty powerful shoulders in my work as a location scout, and I'd learned that once you backed down, once you ceded territory, you were done. I raised my eyebrows. "When we use formal titles at dinner tonight should we call you 'chief?'"

"Of course not." She turned her shoulder to me, an effort to cut me out of the conversation. To Sir Harold, she said, "Needless to say, this isn't going how I'd hoped. However, the reason I'm here is completely aboveboard. I'd hoped to do this discretely, but since it appears that won't be possible...Consortium Hotels Group is interested in Parkview Hall."

A subtle change came over Sir Harold. He didn't move, but his eyes became wary. "Is it?"

"Yes. It is a truly amazing property. We tried to approach you through regular channels, but since we haven't been able to—er—reach you, I decided a personal visit during this house party weekend would be the perfect way to get to know you and broach the subject of acquisition."

"Acquisition?" Sir Harold's manner had definitely shifted. Instead of vague and bemused, he eyed Jo critically. "So you want to purchase it. You're here to make an offer, despite us making it clear that we're not interested in selling."

"We could do amazing things with it, bring it back to its full glory. It would be an exclusive retreat with every luxury. We'd keep the house just as it is. Only slight modifications would be needed."

Out of the corner of my eye, I saw Grace drifting through the room. She went to the table and looked at the butterfly display, but didn't touch anything.

Jo continued speaking, spinning out her pitch. "...and you have so much under-utilized land here. We could capitalize on that, building a resort center that would create jobs for the local economy."

"Hmm…a resort center. That would be a hotel. A high-rise, I presume?"

"No, nothing so gauche as that. We envision a sprawling complex of modern cottages in keeping with the local style that could be rented out for weekends or entire seasons. Of course, transportation links would have to be improved. Bus service is simply not good enough. A rail line would have to be run, but think of the change that would make for Nether Woodsmoor. The industry, the commerce it would draw here. It would be a huge boon for the village."

"And change it completely," Sir Harold said.

Jo removed her phone from her pocket. "I have some artist renderings here. Why don't you take a look?"

"No."

Jo had been speaking smoothly, her voice rolling in gentle waves, but Sir Harold's rather sharp tone halted her, but only for a second. "I'm sure you'll see the benefit, if you consider it. Of course, you and Lady Stone would have a place here as long as you like. I understand you've already moved to the Lodge. We could arrange that it stays in your possession and—"

"No. As we politely informed you, we are not interested in selling. I'm sure you could do amazing things here, but Parkview is a trust, handed down from my father to me, and I'll hand it down to my son. You have wonderful plans I'm sure, but your plans revolve around a bottom line—profitability, correct?"

"Yes, of course."

"And that is why we won't sell to you. Our plans do depend on some profitability, but our bottom line is preservation…of the land, of this house, of the village."

Jo's face was a mixture of perplexity and incomprehension. Sir Harold continued, his voice gentler, "Not everything has to be maximized, modernized, and exploited. I have no doubt that once the paperwork was signed those cottages would transform into something more extensive and intrusive than your present plan, possibly even a high-rise, an idea that I can see even you find a bit repugnant."

"No, I assure you, it won't be like that at all. If you'll just discuss it with Lady Stone…"

"No, my dear. I don't need to. She's in complete agreement with me. Now, if you'll excuse me," he checked his watch. "I believe we all need to dress for dinner."

He left the room, and Jo sent me a furious, tight-lipped look. "That was poorly done. If you hadn't forced my hand, I could have at least chipped away a bit at his reluctance."

"I don't think you can change his mind. He and Beatrice are set on what they want for Parkview."

"Money can change anyone's mind." She swept from the room.

I looked toward Grace, who had watched her leave. "Wow, she's worse than Mrs. Pottering. She's the maths instructor," Grace added.

"Well. At least that answers the question of why her bio and her website listing didn't match. Come on, we better dress for dinner as well."

Michael looked around the doorframe, and seeing that Sir Harold and Jo were gone, he ducked his head and ventured into the room. "Ah—laptop. I'll—ah—just get this."

I motioned toward the door with my head, and Grace followed me out of the room. On the stairs, she looked over the banister at the library door then whispered, "I wanted you to look at his laptop before we left."

"Why?"

"Because he's a spy."

CHAPTER 19

"*A* SPY?" I STUMBLED TO a stop on one of the stairs. Grace grabbed my hand and dragged me up the rest of the steps. "He's coming up behind us."

"Not a James Bond kind of spy," Grace said as soon as I shut the door to the Rose bedroom behind us. "A corporate spy."

"A corporate spy? How do you know about those?"

She gave me a withering look. "Current events reports. I did mine on an article about corporate spying."

"I see. So why do you think Michael is a corporate spy?"

"Because I saw his email. It was on his computer."

She had been wandering around the library while I was focused on Jo and Sir Harold. I did remember Grace had lingered at the table where Sir Harold and Michael had been working.

Grace continued, "It was all there in a long list of things about this weekend—the food, the events, what the bedrooms are like. Even notes about the Wi-Fi. There were lots of pictures attached, but I didn't get to look at them. The email was to Cresthill Towers." She nodded as if that clinched her argument.

"Cresthill Towers," I murmured. "I've heard the name, but can't place it."

"Because it's a big pile on the other side of Upper Benning. My friend Stacy lives near it. When I went home with her during a half-term break last year, her mom and dad took us there for the day. It's not nearly as nice as Parkview. Can I borrow your laptop?"

"Ah—sure," I said.

Grace settled on the bed with my laptop, her fingers racing over the keys.

"He'd left that email open on his computer?" I asked.

Grace wiggled and looked a bit shamefaced. "Well...it was minimized, down at the bottom. That's snooping, and I know it's wrong, but he was in the suspicious pile, so I felt I had to look." She spun the computer around so that I could see a website page. "Now we know why he's been taking all those photos of the house and food and stuff. Corporate espionage," she said with relish.

I sat down beside her and read through the page. Cresthill Towers was undergoing a major renovation and would open to visitors next month, offering daily tours and weekend house party events for exclusive guests. "It does explain Michael taking so many photos, but why would Cresthill Towers feel that they had to send someone in undercover, so to speak? Couldn't they just talk to Sir Harold and Beatrice? Surely they know each other? Why sneak around?"

Grace shrugged.

I closed the laptop. "We'll certainly have several things to tell the DCI Hopkins...whenever he is able to get back." I looked toward the glass doors. The sky was still gray and dark and the rain had tapered off to a light drizzle. I tried to keep my voice upbeat for Grace's sake, but I had the distinct feeling of being stuck in a ditch, going nowhere with wheels spinning away. Sure, we'd discovered some interesting tidbits about the guests, but nothing that changed the situation around Toby Clay's death. We hadn't found out anything that connected anyone in Parkview

Hall to him in the remotest way. And we hadn't found any person who made a better suspect than me.

I repressed a sigh and stood. "We'd better figure out what you're wearing to dinner tonight."

Grace looked down at her droopy t-shirt and baggy jeans. "I don't suppose I can wear this, can I? It's not nearly grand enough."

"No, and it is completely the wrong century. Beatrice made it clear that we did have to dress for dinner, and she wants us in period costumes."

"Oh, I love dressing up. Do you have anything that will fit me?"

"I don't know." I went to the bellpull. "Let's see what Ella can do."

~

"ARE YOU SURE I LOOK OKAY?" Grace asked an hour later, pausing outside the drawing room.

"You look amazing. Remember, Alex said you looked gorgeous."

She made a face. "He's my brother. He has to say that."

"Yes, but it's true."

Ella had been able to find a dress that fit Grace. It was a cream color trimmed in blue. With her hair piled on top of her head, she looked much older than twelve. I'd texted pictures of her to Alex. He'd called me back immediately, first telling Grace how pretty she looked, then he'd asked to speak to me to make sure there weren't any boys her age in the house. "That neckline..." he'd said.

"Is historically accurate," I said with a grin. He'd grumbled some more, and I assured him I'd keep an eye on Grace. I was relegated to the status of chaperone, which was historically accurate, too. During the Regency, a twenty-six-year-old woman

178

would definitely be "on the shelf," which meant her hopes of marrying would have long since faded. Of course, my mother still believed that in the twenty-first century, so maybe things hadn't changed that much.

"Smile," I said. "And watch Beatrice at dinner to see which fork to use," I added as we entered the room.

Beatrice, tonight wearing a mustard yellow silk gown and matching turban, welcomed Grace and exclaimed over how nice she looked then took her around the room, formally introducing her to everyone. Torrie scooted closer to Beth and invited Grace to sit on a sofa beside her. Monique and Beth were bent close together. I noticed that Monique had on a smart black evening dress that was not historically accurate, but it was beautiful. Beatrice must have overlooked Monique's modern dress. Despite the black dress, Monique didn't look like a grieving widow, but she also didn't look like someone who spent her spare time reading classics of English literature either.

Beatrice stopped at the drinks tray, then worked her way around the room to me. She handed me a crystal tumbler. "Try that."

I sipped and nearly did a classic spit take, but managed to swallow instead. Barely.

"It's my own concoction. Regency punch."

I waited for my eyes to stop watering and made a mental note to keep Grace away from the punch bowl.

"Harold told me about the encounter with Jo in the library." Beatrice pushed her slipping turban back above her eyebrows. "Jo is persistent, I'll give her that, but that's all we'll give her."

I followed Beatrice's glance across the room. Jo, wearing another exquisite gown in fuchsia with a gauzy net overlay embroidered with tiny flowers, stood beside Sir Harold, speaking quickly. Jay sat in a chair a few feet away, his attention fixed on the window. I squinted and spotted a thin wire that ran from an ear bud and disappeared into the complicated folds of his cravat. So he was listening to the games, not watching them now.

Sir Harold had a polite expression on his face. He nodded then excused himself to greet Audrey, who had just entered the drawing room.

"So you're not interested in Jo's proposal at all?" I asked Beatrice.

"No, of course not. They approached us a few months ago, requesting a meeting, but that sort of thing doesn't appeal to us. I suppose she thought if she could make her offer in person it would make a difference. I could have saved her a lot of trouble— and expense." Beatrice shook her head and looked fondly at Sir Harold. "He may seem fussy and lost in his own world, but when it comes to Parkview, he has definite ideas. He takes his responsibilities seriously."

"So neither of you think selling to a corporate chain would benefit the village?"

Beatrice sighed and her turban shifted again. "Initially, it would bring in money, but we try to think about these things in the long term. You've seen some of the tourist spots—they're circuses, all show and gloss. Everything becomes a caricature with every aspect of the local economy dependent on tourism. Of course, tourism is part of the economy here now, but it's dependent on the beauty of the land, on nature."

I swirled my drink and thought of the cyclists and the ramblers who descended on Nether Woodsmoor in the spring.

She sighed again. "It may come to that...someday, but not now." She repositioned her turban and grinned. "Of course, I'm wearing a historical costume and entertaining paying guests, so I do realize I could fall into the category of the pot calling the kettle black."

"But you and Sir Harold have the best interests of the village at heart. Your decisions are not made with the bottom line in mind."

She snorted. "True. The accountant and financial advisor have learned not to argue with us. They just shake their heads and mutter now."

"Well, I did discover that another guest is also involved in the hospitality industry."

Beatrice's raised eyebrows disappeared under the edge of her turban.

"Michael. I only have Grace's word on this," I said, warningly. "But she says she saw an email on his laptop today." I described the contents, then said, "So Grace has pegged him as a corporate spy."

Beatrice watched Michael as he strolled across the room toward us. He discretely aimed his phone at the drinks tray and tapped the screen, photographing it, as he went by it.

"I have to say that it does seem slightly more believable than his story about his mother. Surely she isn't *that* interested in the drinks tray?" I said.

"No, I think Grace is probably right. How like Alistair," Beatrice said.

"Alistair?" I asked.

"Alistair Cartwright. He bought Cresthill Towers...oh, a dozen years ago, I think it was. He has a silly competitive nature and thinks everything is a contest. Of course, if he's going to have guests, he wouldn't simply ask us what we do. No, he'd send someone to come in 'undercover.' We'd be happy to share information and tips with him, but he's the sort to think that no matter how open we are, that we'd still hold something back."

Amanda came into the room, spotted Michael, and joined him. He quickly pocketed his phone. She asked him how the research was going as they ambled by us. I missed his short reply, but noticed he wasn't staring at the floor or ducking his head like he usually did. In fact, he was looking at Amanda, a sort of bemused, but dazed expression on his face. "So butterflies...how did you get interested in them?" Amanda asked.

I missed part of his reply, but I did catch the phrase, "...a school project...fascinating."

I raised my eyebrows at Beatrice. She said, "For his sake, I hope he is interested in butterflies. Amanda doesn't seem like the type to put up with a liar."

"No, she doesn't. At least not now," I said, thinking of what Torrie had said about suspecting Amanda had been involved with someone manipulative.

Simon entered the room and came straight toward me. His direct approach was intimidating, but I forced myself not to fall back a step. He was again turned out in Regency finery, wearing his cutaway coat that strained across his biceps, giving him the look of a boy stuffed into clothes he'd outgrown. He ran his finger around the tight neckcloth as he approached. "I'm sorry for letting myself into your room, even if it was unlocked. Audrey," he glanced across the room to his wife. She caught his gaze and dipped her head, indicating he should go on. Simon continued, "she says I press ahead without thinking, and I'm afraid that's what happened today. I shouldn't have accused you like that."

I could read between the lines, and I could tell what he'd left unsaid was that he would still have taken the information to the police, but he was trying to smooth things over so that the evening wasn't awkward. For Beatrice's sake, I said, "Thank you for the apology. I'm sure everything will work out in the end." I said the words, but inside, I wasn't so sure. The suspect list still only contained one name—mine. I may have managed to wiggle out the background on a few guests, but that hadn't widened the suspect pool.

Beatrice put a hand on Simon's arm. "I believe Waverly is pouring you a drink," she said, giving him a way to exit gracefully.

Once he was gone, Beatrice exchanged a look with me. "I heard from the DCI Hopkins this afternoon. He's keeping me updated on the progress of the investigation. Holly's alibi has been confirmed, and he's also spoken with the Clays' doctor. Toby did have a heart condition, and Monique refilled her sleeping pill prescription on Friday morning."

"I don't suppose Hopkins has uncovered someone with a motive to want Toby dead?"

"If he has, he didn't tell me. He did say for me to expect him tomorrow by ten. The forecast for the night is clear, and he expects the river to recede enough that he can make it across the bridge. He told me that we're not to let anyone leave tomorrow until he arrives."

I took a gulp of my drink.

She patted my arm as I shuddered. "I'm sure it will be fine. Ah, there's the signal from Waverly," she said and went off to organize us for the procession into the dining room.

"TORRIE'S FUN," Grace commented later as the ladies exited the dining room and returned to the drawing room.

"Is she?"

"Yes, she played *I spy* with me during one of the courses."

"That was nice of her."

"Yeah, that's what I told her," Grace lowered her voice. "Torrie said it was more fun than talking about dresses with Beth and Monique."

I had thought that dinner might be awkward, but it went smoother than I expected. I was the one who used the wrong fork. Grace followed Beatrice's guide and did fine. The table had again been set with glittering and elegant tableware, but the mood was more informal than the night before. The etiquette barriers were down, and we all ignored the rule of taking turns speaking to only the person on your right or left according to which course was being served. Conversations ranged around the table, and the staff moved unobtrusively, wafting dishes to and fro and expertly keeping our glasses filled. The footmen came and went carrying dishes and trays, but Waverly was a constant presence.

Once we were settled in the drawing room, Waverly appeared with the after dinner tea, coffee, and drinks.

I watched him, directing the rest of the staff with a nod, a lift of his chin, or simply a glance. Grace and I took a seat on one of a pair of sofas that faced each other. Would it be possible to find out more about Waverly? If he was a temporary hire, then the rest of the staff might not know much about him or his background beyond his entertaining circus skills. I could always ask Beatrice what she could find out about him. She probably had hired him through an agency. They might know more. Somehow I didn't think a conversation with him would produce any results. I had a feeling he would look at me with his impassive face—which was rather like Hopkins's expression, come to think of it—and only tell me the barest of information, but I got up from the sofa and crossed the room to him. "Waverly, I'd love to hear more about your time as a magician."

His face was stoic, but he was suddenly busy aligning the crystal decanters. "It was a long time ago. May I pour you a drink or another cup of tea?"

"No, thank you. It is interesting, though. Most people would never guess you could do things like spin plates and juggle spoons."

Waverly gave me a long stare, then said, "Most people see what they expect to see." Thomas stepped into the drawing room and caught Waverly's attention. He said, "If you'll excuse me, miss," and slipped out the door.

I smothered a sigh and returned to the sofa, sitting down beside Grace. Monique and Beth were on the sofa opposite, continuing a discussion of whether it was better to explore the French Riviera by car or boat. Beth said, "We found the most perfect little village inland from Cannes. It would be ideal for a honeymoon, but then I think—no beach in an inland village, and I love the idea of a tropical honeymoon."

"There's always Tahiti," Monique said as she looked away from Beth. She lifted her eyebrows at Waverly, who had returned to the room. He moved to her side instantly. She murmured something to him.

"We could stay in one of those little huts over the water. That would be bliss," Beth said.

"Go to one of the private islands. Less riffraff, if you know what I mean. I'll give you the name of the resort where Toby and I stayed at last year." A pained look came over her face, which surprised me. Since her bout of weeping this morning, she hadn't exhibited any signs of grieving. Intrigued, I watched her, wondering if she was experiencing a momentary pang as she remembered happier times with Toby, or was she grieving, but not showing any outward signs of it. Private grief didn't seem to go with the public personality she'd cultivated over the years, mugging for the cameras and courting coverage with her outrageous life choices.

Monique took out her black envelope clutch and removed a pill bottle. "They have a sublime spa there." She removed the lid and tipped a single pill, which must be her nightly sleeping pill, into her hand then took the tumbler of water from the silver tray that Waverly had returned with. She downed the medicine and returned the glass to the tray without looking at Waverly, not missing a beat in the conversation. "Open air spas near the cliffs and tropical pools. Very nice."

Distantly, I was aware that the double doors opened. The men filtered into the room. Waverly returned, poured drinks for them, then stepped out into the hall, closing the doors behind him, probably staying out of my way so I couldn't ask him more awkward questions. I noticed Waverly's quick exit, but it only vaguely registered. I was thinking about Monique. Something pulled at the edge of my thoughts, bothering me about the last moments...what was it? Something about that pill. She'd been so low-key about it tonight. Not like last night. Last night, she had been—what?—more showy, almost theatrical...

Grace pulled me out of my reverie. She twisted around on the sofa to speak to Amanda, who was carrying a teacup as she moved along the back of the sofa. "I saw your slackline today when we were in your room. Do you think you'll set it up tomorrow before you leave, if it's not raining?"

Amanda paused and gripped the back of the sofa with her free hand. Despite the dimness of the room, which was again lit only by candlelight, I could see her face clearly as the color had faded from her cheeks. "Um—I'm sorry, but I don't know what you're talking about."

"You know, slackline. The flat webbing. You put some in a box," Grace said.

"No, I didn't," Amanda said, her voice sharp. "You must have seen something else."

"No, I know what it is. I saw the label on it and everything. My friend's brother had some. I tried slacklining and liked it. I want to do it again." Grace twisted around and looked my way. "You saw it, too, didn't you, Kate?"

I glanced from Grace to Amanda. Amanda's chest, so visible in the low cut gown, was moving up and down with her rapid breathing. Her eyes were wide with fear, I realized. Suddenly, I knew exactly what Grace was talking about. I *had* seen the rope, but I'd thought it was a belt. It had been flat, like a nylon tie down, but I'd only seen the end of it as Amanda stuffed it into a cardboard box.

Thoughts zipped through my mind. Torrie and Beth teasing Amanda about her weird hobbies. A slackline in the same color as the natural stone of Parkview Hall. The strange clear stripes on the balusters. Amanda spilling her tea when I had half-jokingly said that someone must have levitated onto the balcony.

Could that be the answer? Had Amanda somehow rigged a slackline between her balcony and the balcony of the Mahogany bedroom, crossed it during the night, and killed Toby?

I looked back at Grace, giving her a warning shake of my head, but she wasn't looking my way.

There was a natural lull in the conversation, and Grace's words drew everyone's attention as she said, "My brother thinks slacklining is dangerous. Maybe you could talk to him when he comes to pick me up tomorrow..." she faltered to a stop as the expression on Amanda's face finally registered. Grace shot me a puzzled look.

I cleared my throat, and tried to think of something innocuous to say. We still had the rest of the evening and the night to get through before the police would, hopefully, be back. "The Versailles bedroom is quite a sight," I said into the quietness of the room.

Everyone had picked up on the tension radiating from Amanda. Michael had taken a seat on one of a pair of small decorative chairs, but he tensed, poised to stand as he watched Amanda.

Amanda closed her eyes for a second then looked my way. "It's no use, Kate. I can't keep it secret any longer. I should have known I couldn't keep it quiet."

"Secret?" Beatrice asked. "What secret is that?"

"That I slacklined across the courtyard last night and broke into the Mahogany bedroom."

CHAPTER 20

$\mathcal{A}$ SECOND OF SILENCE FOLLOWED Amanda's words, then several people began talking at once. Michael jumped up so quickly that his chair tumbled over. "That can't be true," he said, his voice carrying over the din.

Grace sent me an anguished look. She looked like a bird poised on a wire, ready to fly away in an instant. The last thing I wanted was for Grace to leave the room. To get to the door, she'd have to go right by Amanda. Amanda! My thoughts stuck there. I never would have thought she was the murderer. I motioned for Grace to stay where she was.

"Perhaps you'd better tell us about it," Beatrice said. "Keeping secrets hardly ever turns out well, in my experience. Much better to get it out in the open."

Amanda carefully put her teacup down on a nearby table, then after a quick glance at Monique, she focused on the back of the sofa. "I…knew Toby," she said simply.

Her words brought back to mind this afternoon when she'd said the police suspecting me had been foolish because I hadn't known Toby. I completely missed the easy use of his first name, but now as she said his name again, I picked up on it—the familiarity of her tone.

Monique sensed it too. "You," she said incredulously. "You were Toby's old lover?" She ran her gaze over Amanda in a dismissive way. "A cook? No wonder he dropped you." She seemed to realize that the rest of us were staring at her, and she added, "Before we arrived, Toby told me one of the guests had been his lover. He was cruel that way. But if I'd known it was you," she glanced back at Amanda then flicked a hand, "well, clearly, I wasted a few minutes worrying. I needn't have." She propped her elbow on her knee and leaned forward, chin in her palm as if she were setting up to listen to a good story. "So you killed him because he ignored you?"

"No." Amanda's voice was scandalized. "No, I did not kill him. He had...something of mine that I wanted back. He wouldn't give it back. In fact," she blew out a long breath then said, "There's no point in keeping anything back now." She looked at Beatrice. "As you said about secrets—they're dangerous things." She raised her chin and looked down at Monique. "Yes, Toby and I had an affair. It began two months after your wedding."

Monique looked like she'd been punched in the stomach, but Amanda hurried on, the words flowing out of her more quickly. "I wasn't proud of it. In fact, I hated myself while it was going on. I didn't mean for it to happen. He came to the hotel often, on business. Our paths crossed a few times, and I—well, it happened." She was back to looking at the sofa. "I felt horrible and ended it, but I had done a foolish thing. I made him mad. He didn't like it that I broke it off. Toby had always insisted that we keep everything quiet. Very discreet. No emails, no phone calls, no texts. And I went along with him...except once. I wrote him a note, a letter. He kept it. And then about three months ago, he happened to be on the same bus as I was on the way home. I'm sure it wasn't an accident. He never takes the bus. He told me he still had the letter. If I didn't pay him several hundred pounds, he'd show it to my boss. I'd be fired, and Toby threatened to make sure I wouldn't get a reference."

Beatrice said softly, "But surely he didn't need the money?"

"No, of course not. It was all a game of manipulation with him. He was angry with me and wanted to make me pay emotionally. To make me worry and fret. He wanted to control me." Amanda shot a look of pity at Monique. Monique looked away at the ceiling then said, "Yes. He was like that. Cruel, as I said."

"So anyway." Amanda ran her finger along a seam in the sofa. "Once I received the welcome packet with the guest list, I knew he would be here. And when I saw the map of the house, well, I knew if I could get into his room, I could get the letter back. That night on the bus, he'd shown it to me. He had folded it into a tiny square and kept it in a leather business card holder that he carried everywhere with him. I knew he might have another copy of it somewhere," she frowned, "but I didn't think he did. It wasn't like it was that important—to him, anyway. To me, it was a huge deal, but to him, it was just a way to toy with me. And once I'd seen that he still had the letter...well, that was all the leverage he'd need, wasn't it? So I figured if I could at least get back the original, then I might be free of the threat. It was a chance I decided I had to take. If I stole the letter, and he had another copy, well, it would come out anyway, but at least if I made the attempt to get the letter and it was the only copy, then I wouldn't have to live with the continual worry that he could reveal it at any time. I couldn't believe my crazy idea worked, but it did. There were so many things that had to come together, but everything went off without a hitch."

We all were stunned, I think because there were a few seconds of silence then Simon said, "Sounds like a perfect motive for murder."

"I know," Amanda said. "I knew that's exactly what it would seem like, but I swear I did not kill him. He was already dead when I got there."

CHAPTER 21

$\mathcal{A}$MANDA SAID, "I KNOW YOU probably won't believe me, but he was already...gone when I got in the room." She gripped the sofa, her gaze darting around the room. "I know it sounds unbelievable, but it's true. I didn't kill him. In fact, I didn't even go near him, at first, anyway. Once I was in the room, I listened to make sure it was quiet. I heard breathing, deep and even breathing, and the bed had those curtains around it, so I couldn't see much. I crept around the room, looking for the leather envelope."

I wondered how she had gotten the hook and eye unlatched, but she was speaking quickly, and I didn't want to interrupt her.

"I found the leather case on the top of the dresser along with some change and slips of paper. I took out the letter and then headed back for the windows, but as I went by the bed, I saw his face through a gap in the bed curtains and I knew..." her voice faltered. She took a deep breath then said, "I just knew. It was horrible. And at the same moment, it hit me that I had put myself in an even worse situation."

Amanda glanced at Monique. "I'm sure I stood there for at least a minute or two, debating what to do. With you there, out cold beside him…" Amanda shivered, "…it was awful. All I could think of to do was to get out of there and keep quiet. There was no reasonable excuse or explanation for me being inside that room. I wasn't even sleeping in the same wing so I couldn't use the excuse that I'd somehow stumbled into the wrong room. There was nothing else I could do, except leave."

Amanda shrugged, a miserable look on her face. "So that's what I did. I felt terrible doing it, but I went back across the courtyard on the slackline. I unfastened it, then pulled it across. I'd rigged up a way to use a guideline to get it in place, but once I unhooked it, I knew the trailing end would leave a mark across the courtyard, but it was faint. I could barely see it in the morning. The groundskeeper washed it away before the police arrived. They were only interested in footprints anyway. I knew Toby's death would be discovered in the morning, but I was afraid that Monique might wake during the night and realize…so I stayed awake most of the night then made sure I was in the vicinity of the other wing most of the morning. As soon as I heard Monique scream, I rushed up there and barged in with everyone else. It was such a confusing scene that I was able to slip out to the balcony and get the anchor for the slackline that I'd had to leave in place. I stuffed it inside my shirt and went back to my room to hide it, but I knew I needed to get rid of it."

Amanda smiled sadly at me. "Grace's eyes were too sharp. I thought the police might search our belongings tomorrow before they let us leave, and since I didn't want to be caught carrying several feet of slackline and a harness through the house, I decided to pack them. I taped up the box and gave it to Thomas earlier today. I asked him to see that it was posted to my home address. I'm sure the police will be able to find it. It's probably in a stack somewhere to be sent off in tomorrow's post."

There were many gaps in her story, questions I wanted to ask, but as weird and crazy as her story was, I believed her. Who would make up a story like that? It was so far-fetched, yet just within the edge of possibility.

"She's lying." Monique jumped up, and her envelope clutch tumbled to the floor as she appealed to Beatrice. "She should be locked up until the police can get here. She killed Toby. It *had* to be her. You all heard her. She had a reason to want him dead."

When Monique's clutch hit the floor, the latch released, spilling the contents at my feet: a pill bottle, a phone, and a lipstick tube. The contents were different from last night when I'd seen inside her purse. What was different? Then it hit me. Waverly's words seemed to echo in my mind. *People see what they expect to see.*

"Those weren't sleeping pills," I said, softly to myself as I worked it out in my head. Things shifted, sliding into place, and I knew what had happened.

Monique stood with her hands braced on her hips, but at my voice, her head snapped toward me. "Of course they were."

I gulped, wishing I'd kept the thought to myself, but at least I was surrounded by people. "Yes, I'm sure they were *tonight*. It was last night that they weren't."

"What are you talking about? Everyone saw me take a sleeping pill last night."

"Did we?" I licked my lips and felt an internal quiver. Her face was so adamant and set. But then I thought of yesterday, her spat with Toby and the trash Ella had emptied today. "Or did we see you take something that looked like a sleeping pill after dinner? Something like a mint, perhaps?"

Monique hesitated for a second before sputtering as she stepped so close that she loomed over me, but I kept talking. "Mints would be perfect, wouldn't they? With their similar color and shape, they could easily pass as sleeping pills, at least at a casual glance. You could take one here in the drawing room, and we'd all be your witnesses that you couldn't have murdered your husband. All you had to do was dump the mints when you got back to your room—after Toby took one of your real sleeping pills, and you suffocated him, I assume. You could flush the mints and refill the medicine bottle with the real sleeping pills, which you'd kept in the mint package. Very clever, that. You knew the staff would have access to your belongings and two bottles of pills—a real one and a fake one—might be noticed, but hiding one set of pills in a mint package was smart. People see what they expect to see, don't they? If there are white round tablets in a mint package, then they must be mints. White round tablets in a pill bottle must be pills."

Monique was breathing quickly and shallowly through her nose, her hands clenched at her side. "This is ridiculous." She tossed her head and looked first at Beatrice then Sir Harold. "Are you going to let her speak to me this way? She's obviously insane."

I licked my lips, glancing around for something that I could put between her and me, in case she lunged at me, which she looked like she wanted to do. The fringed pillow beside my thigh wouldn't help me, and the decorative bowl on the table between the sofas, which besides probably being a valuable antique, was too far away to reach.

"That's why you wouldn't give Toby a mint yesterday when he asked for one," I plowed on. Better to get it all out there. "I thought it was an example of how far apart you were as a couple—you wouldn't even give him a mint!—but you *couldn't* give him one because they weren't mints at all. They were your sleeping pills. If you gave one to Toby at that point, he'd know immediately from the taste that they weren't mints. No one would think twice if they saw them, and after you'd made the switch and put them in the pill bottle, the police would assume you couldn't have murdered Toby. Of course, you must have given him a sleeping pill after you returned to your room and made the switch, which would make it so much easier to kill him."

"I can't believe you've let her go on with this obviously ludicrous story. You don't even have any proof."

"There's a trash bag somewhere still on this property with an empty mint package. I saw it when Ella cleaned the Mahogany bedroom today. I know some people consume quite a few mints, but I haven't seen you pop one in your mouth. Are you saying you ate a whole package between yesterday and today? And I wonder what the police will find when they dig into your finances? How were Toby's finances set up? Do you inherit? Was he really supportive of your efforts to branch out into being a television hostess? You've told us yourself that he was cruel. It sounds as if he'd be just the type of person to tell the press one thing—that he supported your business ideas—but do just the opposite. Was he cutting off his support for your business ventures...like the perfume deal?"

Monique was visibly trembling. I was sure it was with rage, not fear. I gripped the fringed cushion and inched away from Grace. Surely, Monique wouldn't attack me in a room full of witnesses? She quivered there for a moment, sending me a look of pure hatred, then she darted for the door. I'd been poised to move, and I jumped up, but had no desire to follow her. I was around the sofa in two strides, moving away from the door toward the wall. I yanked on the bellpull. "Someone stop her," I called, but no one had been standing in the path to the door.

Michael lunged for her, but she sidestepped him.

Monique was only a few steps from the door. Simon stepped on the trailing hem of her dress, but she only clawed the material out from under his foot in a second. She turned back toward the door, but as she whirled with a burst of speed, Waverly opened one of the double doors, smacking Monique squarely in the face.

Sir Harold shouted, "Stop her! She's the murderer."

Monique fell backward, clutching her nose, then tried to slip around Waverly, but he caught her, wrapping his arms around her waist from behind as if he was going to give her the Heimlich maneuver. She was taller than Waverly, kicking and thrashing and clawing at his hands, but he lifted her a few feet off the floor and held her tight.

"Perhaps I should escort Mrs. Clay to the Green bedroom?" Waverly asked, his tone bland. "It has a secure lock."

CHAPTER 22

*A*FTER A LONG, BUT UNEVENTFUL night in which Grace slept on a cot in the Rose bedroom with me, Sunday had dawned clear and cloudless with no trace of the rain that had drenched the countryside except for the squishy earth and swollen river. Monique had spent the night locked in the luxurious Green bedroom, apparently on the phone with lawyers, because her team of solicitors arrived via a helicopter that touched down on one of the meadows not far from Parkview, disturbing the sheep on the distant rolling hills, so that they trotted away, their puffy outlines disappearing over the swell of ground. Because it didn't rain again during the night, the water receded, and Hopkins and his team were able to cross the bridge, arriving in time to meet the team of solicitors on the gravel in front of Parkview. Alex had beaten both the lawyers and the law, crossing the bridge at first light with the water still sloshing calf-deep over his Wellington boots.

Watching from the windows inside the house, the meeting between the solicitors and Hopkins's people looked tense. I thought we might be about to witness something similar to a rugby scrum, but Hopkins must have been able to sort everything out because soon he was in the library calling people in one at a time for interviews.

I wasn't surprised I was one of the first people called. Jo asked that she and Jay be interviewed first because they had a flight to catch. After being closeted with Hopkins for about fifteen minutes, I had a brief glimpse of them as they motored out of the library. Jo gave me a sharp nod and sailed on, Jay ambling along in her wake, his attention focused on his phone. Thomas followed them across the entry with their bags.

My interview with Hopkins was actually fairly short. Monique wasn't the only one on the phone last night. Hopkins had spoken to me by phone and had taken me through exactly what had happened in the drawing room. Today, with his face as blank as Waverly's he again went over everything I'd told him on the phone about discovering that Jo and Michael were at Parkview under false pretenses then about how I'd put together the scraps and bits about Monique. When I finished, he removed a sealed plastic bag from an interior pocket of his jacket. "Is this the mint container that you saw emptied from Mrs. Clay's trash?"

He handed it to me, and I turned it over. "It looks like it. It's the same brand, but I suppose it could be from someone else."

He nodded and took the bag back. "There is some residue in the package. We will have it tested. If it is a medical compound instead of simply dust off a breath mint it will help our case. Thank you, Ms. Sharp. You may go."

I half stood. I had expected to be grilled, taken back and forth over the events of the last days. I sat back down, perching on the edge of the chair. "So, just to be clear, I'm no longer a suspect?"

"No, Ms. Sharp, certainly not now. You were not a good candidate to begin with. No motive and no connection to the victim that I could find. You were a last minute addition to the house party. When I looked at the larger picture, I suspected that you were involved purely because of propinquity. The hairpin could have been left at an earlier time, by a different guest as your friend pointed out to me. Or, it could have been an impulsive effort on Mrs. Clay's part to throw suspicion your way when she realized the investigation wasn't going as she thought it would. With your door unlocked, she would have had the opportunity to slip inside your room sometime after her interview with me, take a hairpin and toss it from your balcony to hers." He paused and leaned back in the chair. "Have you heard of Occam's razor?"

"Yes," I said slowly. "Something about the simplest answer is usually right."

"Correct. This case appeared highly complicated, but it wasn't. A wife wanted to be free of her husband and murdered him in a way that she hoped would be overlooked."

"What? She thought that the asphyxiation wouldn't be noticed?"

"Research is apparently not Mrs. Clay's strong suit. She is, of course, not talking at the moment, but from statements made yesterday, I think that she drugged her husband then suffocated him, thinking that we would assume that his medical condition had caused his death."

"She didn't realize that suffocation would leave traces...evidence?"

"Not everyone is an aficionado of crime novels or television shows...or even Internet research, it seems," he said with a shake of his head. "Of course, most criminals are not secret masterminds. As in Mrs. Clay's case. She was simply greedy and rather naive when it came to modern investigative techniques."

"I guess she should have read more Arthur Conan Doyle and less D. H. Lawrence," I said to myself.

"I'm sorry?"

"Never mind. She has lived in her own world, behaving as she pleased, with her family bailing her out of all her past scrapes. She probably thinks this will be no different."

Hopkins showed more animation than I'd ever seen as he said

firmly, "She's wrong this time. This is murder." He stood and escorted me to the door, subsiding back into his bland manner. "Interesting case, though."

"Yes," I said. "An accidental locked room mystery."

"As I said, there's always a simple solution."

"THIS IS GOING to be so cool," Grace said. She stood beside me, one hand shading her eyes.

Grace and I, along with several of the guests stood on the balcony of the Versailles bedroom. Several of the staff were lingering in the courtyard and at windows. Amanda was busy with the flat webbed rope, which looked more like what I would have called a rope tie down, but Grace had informed me that it was the most popular brand of slackline rope.

"I don't think she's going to actually go across," I said.

"I know," Grace said, her voice tinged with disappointment. "But at least we'll get to see how she did it."

I looked down at her sharply. There was something in her tone that made me think she was filing all the details away for a future reenactment. I nudged Alex, who stood beside me and whispered, "Grace's boarding school doesn't have a courtyard like this, does it?"

"No," Alex said, slowly. "But I think I'll have a chat with the headmistress when I return with Grace after the break."

Amanda had set the anchor around the back baluster on the Mahogany bedroom's balcony. The color of the slackline was so similar to the stone that it was hard to distinguish it from the stone. "Okay, the guideline is in place." She plucked a line so thin that it was barely visible.

"I can hardly see it," Alex said.

"I know," I agreed. "If I squint, I can just make it out. Of course, if I'd noticed it the other day, I would have just assumed it was supposed to be there—that it was something that had been put in place by Parkview's staff."

The guideline ran in a loop from Amanda's balcony to the anchor set-up on the Mahogany balcony then back to Amanda. She attached the end of the guideline to the slackline and then pulled the guideline. The slackline inched across the courtyard. "Once it's through the carabiner on the other side, then it's just a matter of getting it back to this side." Amanda kept pulling until the slackline had made the complete circuit.

Once it was within reach, she untied the guideline then slipped another carabiner onto the slackline. "This is a clove hitch knot to hold this carabiner in place," she said. "Then it's a matter of looping the slackline back and forth between this single carabiner and the two that I have at the anchor on this side," she said with a nod of her head at the two carabiners, which were attached to an anchor line looped around the baluster on her balcony. She deftly worked the slackline back and forth between the metal clips. "Now, I just pull." She grabbed the trailing slackline, giving it several firm tugs, pulling the saggy line taut. "Then it's all about balance. I used a harness, of course," she added. "I attached it to the slackline in case I had any slip-ups."

Grace had watched the whole thing intently and now was looking at the pile of guideline that Amanda had discarded once the slackline was pulled across the courtyard. "How did you get this across?" Grace asked, fingering the thin line.

"I arrived early on Friday and attached it to my balcony then spent a lot of time in the courtyard." She shook her head. "Everyone kept asking me if I needed anything, wanting to bring me tea. When I finally got a moment alone, I grabbed the line, which I'd let fall into the courtyard, raced across to stand under the Mahogany bedroom's balcony, then tossed it up there. It took me three tries to get it on there. I was so glad no one came out. Anyway, after it was up there, I went up to the Mahogany bedroom and set up the anchor, looped the guideline through it, then dropped the guideline down into the courtyard again. None of the other guests had arrived at that point so the doors to the bedrooms were open because the staff was putting the last minute touches on them—flowers and that sort of thing. I was able to sneak in and out without anyone seeing me. Then I only had to wait around for another time when the courtyard was deserted and toss it back up on my balcony and tighten it so that it wasn't trailing across the ground."

"Wow, that's a lot of work," Grace said.

"Yes, but I was motivated," Amanda said sadly. She shook her head at Grace. "Never put yourself in a position that you don't want people to know what you're doing. You make yourself vulnerable."

"It's amazing that it worked," I said, eyeing the courtyard and the windows overlooking it. "How could someone not have noticed?"

Amanda ran a hand over her forehead. "I don't know. I was incredibly lucky, but when I set up the other guests hadn't arrived, and if the staff noticed me at all they probably thought I was doing some sort of strange workout," she said with a small grin. "Anyway, it all went so well, I couldn't believe it, actually. There were so many things that had to come together. Besides getting the guideline and the anchors in place, I had two sleeping pills that I'd ground up. I had to make sure that Monique and Toby wouldn't wake up while I was prowling around their room. I managed to tip the powder into her tea when we were all handing the drinks around after dinner, but I couldn't get close to Toby's drink. When he said he'd take a sleeping pill later, I had to hope he would. But then Monique took her 'sleeping pill.' I didn't want to overdose her, so I managed to bump into her and make her spill her tea. Finally, I had to make sure Beth and Torrie were out, too." She looked at them and grimaced. "I'm sorry. I put sleeping pills in your hot chocolate."

Beth stood inside the balcony doors in the Versailles bedroom her arms crossed, a sulky expression on her face, probably because all the attention was on Amanda, not her. She only shrugged, but Torrie, who was testing the tension of the slackline, said, "No worries. It was the best night's sleep I've had since I ran that half-marathon."

One thing still bothered me. "But how did you get the glass doors open? And how did you refasten the lock?"

"When I went into the Mahogany bedroom to set the anchor, I took this with me." She pulled a hefty piece of metal out of her pocket. "It's a magnet, a rather heavy-duty one. I ran it over the hook to magnetize it. It's such a strong magnet that even when I held it on the other side of the closed door, I could move the hook with it."

"Can I see it?" Grace asked.

"Sure. You can even try it on our doors. I tested it on them. If Beth will just close the door and latch them..."

Beth stepped back and looked rather happy to lock us all outside.

Amanda pointed to the area of the doorframe where the hook was attached on the inside of the door. "Put the magnet here and then lift it up and circle it around."

Grace followed her instructions. In a second, the edge of the hook appeared in the pane of glass as it followed the magnet as Grace moved it in an arc. "And there you go." Amanda pushed the door open and stepped inside. "Locking it back is trickier, but I got it done, even with my shaking hands. I didn't want any detail to give away the fact that I'd been in the Mahogany bedroom."

"But surely if the letter was gone, he'd suspect you," I said.

"Yes, but there was the chance that he wouldn't realize the letter was gone until later. But even if he noticed it right away, what could he do? If he told Lady Stone or Sir Harold something had been stolen from his room, they would ask what it was, and he wouldn't want to tell them it was a blackmail letter."

"Can I try the magnet trick again?" Grace asked.

"Certainly." Amanda stepped outside. "Let's see if you can get it back in the eye portion, the catch."

Grace went to work, her forehead wrinkled in concentration.

"How did you know that the doors would have this sort of hook and eye catch? What if they had proper locks?" Simon asked. He's spent the last few minutes standing in the back corner of the balcony, his posture of crossed arms similar to Beth's.

"I knew they had these locks. Parkview has photos of all their guest rooms on their website. Once I had the welcome packet with the guest list and room assignments, all I had to do was go online and download the images of the rooms. They were high-resolution images, thank goodness, so I could enlarge them and look at every detail, down to the catch on the window."

"You were thorough, but you were lucky, too." Simon shook his head. "I wouldn't want to play cards with you."

"Got it," Grace said and tried the door. It was locked back in place. "Now I'll unlock it." She had it unlatched in seconds and opened the door just as Audrey approached.

Audrey leaned around the door. "Hello, everyone. Looks like I missed the demonstration, but I know Simon will tell me all about it." It was the first time I'd seen her in modern clothing, and I almost didn't recognize her in a plain black t-shirt, white capri pants, and loafers. Her gaze traveled around the balcony. "There you are, Simon. Mrs. King is waiting for us in the kitchen. She found a schematic of how the water was originally piped to the house from the river. If you want to take a look before we leave, we should go now."

"Yes, I want to see that. It could give me some ideas for our set-up." He crossed the balcony to her.

"If we don't see you again before we leave, it was lovely to meet you all," Audrey said then linked her hand through Simon's arm.

As they crossed the room to the door, I heard her ask him, "How was the demonstration?"

"Interesting...of course, I thought she might be involved."

She tapped his arm. "No, you did not. You had that other nice young lady, Kate, pegged as the murderer."

"But Amanda was a close second in my book."

"No, I was the one who said that there was more to that tea spilling than met the eye. Perhaps I should go with you on every case. You have been making noises about hiring an assistant..."

I exchanged a glance with Alex, and he said, "Probably the best business decision Simon could ever make."

"In a few years, she'll probably be the lead detective, and Simon can pursue his real passion—prepping."

"Prepping for what?" Alex asked.

"It's a long story. Let me say goodbye to Amanda, and I'll tell you about it."

I moved to the back of the balcony where Amanda was disassembling her slackline. "What does Hopkins say about your breaking and entering?"

Amanda blew out a long breath. "He certainly didn't approve of it, but once he had the whole story, he said that in the big picture of what happened this weekend, it was a small thing. He's not even going to take the letter into evidence. So I'm free," she said with a big smile. "It's been embarrassing and traumatic, but I can go on now."

Torrie threw her arm around Amanda's shoulders. "And no more mean, unavailable men, right?"

"No, I'm done with that." Amanda shot a glance across the balcony to where Michael had been standing the whole time. A faint blush crept up her face when Michael smiled at her. "I think I'll aim for a much less complicated relationship next time."

"Ah—Amanda," I paused and glanced uncertainly between her and Michael. It wasn't my place to give away his secret, but...

Amanda put her hand on my arm. "Don't worry. I already

know. He told me last night after everything calmed down. He said he didn't want to have any secrets from me."

"So you're okay with him sneaking around?"

"Well, he decided he's done with corporate spying. He's actually the catering manager at Cresthill Towers. Alistair Cartwright only picked him to come here this weekend because Michael is interested in butterflies. And Sir Harold isn't upset. In fact, he and Michael have decided to collaborate on a book about famous vintage butterfly collections."

"That's great. I'm glad it all worked out." I looked toward the Versailles bedroom where Beth was sitting by herself flipping through a bridal magazine. "What about Beth? *She* seems a little upset."

"She'll get over it," Amanda said easily. "Once we're back to talking about wedding dresses, she'll be fine."

Grace came over and held out the magnet to Amanda. "Thanks for letting me try it."

"Why don't you keep it?" Amanda said. "I don't have any use for it now, thank goodness."

TEN MINUTES LATER, I zipped my suitcase closed. Alex and Grace were waiting for me outside on Parkview's front steps. Ella had offered to help me pack, but I'd told her I could do it myself, and it had only taken me a few minutes. I put my hands on my hips and took one last look around the room. It was still a beautiful room. I was glad I'd been able to stay in Parkview, but I was actually looking forward to returning to my cozy little cottage.

Ella was shifting through the gorgeous dresses, stacking them on the bed in piles so that they could be cleaned before the next house party. "Thank you for everything you've done Ella—I mean Tewkesbury." Although all the guests were back in casual modern clothes, the staff was still maintaining the stiff formality of historical dress and accompanying reserve.

She bobbed a curtsy. "It was my pleasure, Kate—er, I mean Miss Sharp." She rotated her shoulders. "I'm sorry, but I've had it. I can't remember who to call what. I'm tired of scurrying around answering bells and curtsying." She slapped her hand over her mouth and looked toward the open door, afraid someone might have overheard. Then she removed her hand and said in a low voice, "I'm sorry, I shouldn't have said anything."

I leaned toward her. "You know, I don't blame you. You don't have to curtsy to me anymore. Consider yourself off-duty around me. A servant's life must have been awfully tiring, but wasn't it just for you to practice staying in character?"

"Yes, but I didn't like it much. It hasn't been at all like I imagined. When I worked during the last house party I was in training and spent a lot of time following another maid around, watching her. I thought this time it would be like being in a play, but it was...well, so much work, actually. I barely had time to think about how Tewkesbury—that's how I thought of my character, you know—how Tewkesbury the maid would feel, what her motivation would be, how she would react. Perhaps acting isn't my thing at all."

"It would be different if it were a play instead of working a job during a long weekend. Will you still try for the drama school?"

"I don't know. I'm not sure now. I'm not sure what I want to do. I love Louise, but I don't want to work at the White Duck forever. If I have another go at this acting thing and still hate it, I'll have to find something else."

"Well, perhaps you could try for a local production, and if that doesn't work out, I know that Beatrice is looking for a new publicity director. You could always apply for that."

"Shall I take your bag down for you, Miss Sharp?" asked a masculine voice from beside me, and I jumped.

"Thomas, I didn't hear you."

"That's my job, miss. Your bag?"

"Yes, please take it down," I said, thinking that I'd enjoy one last luxury and let someone else carry my bag. "Good luck, Ella. Keep me updated." I pressed a tip into her hand. I'd asked Beatrice and found out that it was appropriate to tip the staff when one left a house party.

"Okay," she said and waved instead of curtsying.

I followed Thomas downstairs and gave a solemn nod to Waverly as he held the door open for me. "Goodbye, Waverly. Thank you for everything."

"It was a pleasure meeting you, Miss Sharp," he said in his normal expressionless tone, but as I went out the door, I gave him one last smile as I handed him a tip. I was almost sure I saw a wink.

Beatrice was talking with Alex and Grace at the base of one set of the curving staircases. Thomas, his back straight, his white wig glowing in the sunshine, marched to them.

"You can leave it here, Thomas," I said and thanked him, slipping him a tip before he bowed and made his sedate return trip up the stairs.

I turned to Beatrice, "It has been quite a weekend."

"Yes, I'm afraid this house party will become as infamous as some of the other house parties that have been given here, although nothing could match the seventh baronet's celebration of the completion of the east wing." Beatrice glanced toward Grace, who was dragging her toe through the gravel drive. "But that is a subject for another day." Beatrice turned and ran her gaze over the front of the house. "It didn't work out quite like we expected, did it?"

"No. I'm sorry I wasn't able to help you more with the poison pen posts."

"You did figure out who was behind them," Beatrice said.

"But not in a discreet way."

"No, but that couldn't be helped. At least it's all cleared up, and Hopkins has told me he will do his best to keep things as quiet as possible. Although, we've already had a few calls asking when the 'murder room' will be available."

"Well, I think it was an absolutely smashing weekend," Grace said. "That's what my friend Stacy would say, absolutely smashing. It was better than an old game of Cluedo," Grace said with a sidelong glance at Alex.

He tweaked a strand of her hair. "Probably a good idea to keep your sleuthing to mystery novels in the future."

"I'm glad you enjoyed it," Beatrice said to Grace, "and I hope you'll come back to visit next time you're in Nether Woodsmoor. I'll show you the cellars. Nice and damp and creepy."

"Sounds wonderful."

We said goodbye to Beatrice, and I reached for my suitcase handle, but Alex picked it up first. "Allow me. After being cosseted and pampered, I'll ease you back into real life."

"Since the weekend included being accused of murder, I'm ready to get back to real life."

"Glad to hear it," Alex said with a steady look that made me feel like I was the only woman in the world. "I missed you."

"I missed you too," I said seriously. Then before the moment got too intense, I said, "Believe me, there were many times when I wished you were there. And not just so I could have seen you in Regency breeches."

We paused on the soggy bridge, Alex in the middle and Grace and me on each side. We watched the water rush by as it swirled and bubbled, barely skimming along the bottom stones of the underside of the bridge. After a few minutes, I pressed away from the bridge. "Well, I have a report to write for Elise. I should head home."

"Right," Alex said. "That's one research report I actually *want* to read." He picked up my suitcase. "We'll let you get at it."

Grace's mouth turned down. "Oh. I'd kind of hoped that we might go to the ruins. You know," she looked at Alex quickly then concentrated on the river. "All of us. I mean, if you want to, Kate."

"I don't know," Alex said. "It'll be wet. And you put up such a fuss before," he added, but I could tell he was pleased. "What was it you called them, something about stupid old ruins, I think?"

Grace merely rolled her eyes and looked at me. "Want to, Kate?"

I reached for Alex's free hand. "I'd love to."

THE END

~

Stay up to date with with Sara. Sign up for her updates and get exclusive content and giveaways.

~

Don't miss Kate and Alex's next adventure, a scouting trip to Bath, England. Death in an Elegant City is available in ebook, print, and audio.

Sightseeing can be murder . . .

Location scout Kate Sharp is thrilled to be part of a scouting trip to the historic city of Bath, England to research the location for a Jane Austen documentary. But before Kate gets a chance to stroll the elegant boulevards where Austen once lived, murder cuts the sightseeing short.

Now Kate must rearrange her itinerary and find the killer before she and the production are shut down permanently.

Perfect for fans of British detective mysteries, Death in an Elegant City blends the puzzle of a whodunit with the mystique of Jane Austen. It is the forth installment in the popular Murder on Location series, a collection of traditional British cozy mysteries. Escape into a quintessentially English cozy with a Sara Rosett mystery today!

THE STORY BEHIND THE STORY

Thanks for reading *Death in a Stately Home*. Kate and Alex will encounter another mystery soon. If you'd like to know when I have a new book out, you can sign up for my updates at Rosett.-com/signup/2, which also gives you access to exclusive excerpts of upcoming books as well as members-only giveaways.

This book was so much fun to research, yet one of the hardest to write. I loved delving into all the Regency etiquette, manners, food, and clothes. My Pinterest page for *Death in a Stately Home* is evidence of how much I enjoyed it. It was research. Really. Take a look for Regency fashion and food as well as a dose of stately homes and other places that inspired me as I wrote.

The idea for writing a mystery set during an English house party was irresistible—I'm a sucker for any type of mystery set at a grand estate—and there just aren't enough of those kinds of books in my opinion, so I was so excited to write one. If you have a favorite British manor house mystery, I'd love to hear about it.

The idea of a locked room mystery intrigued me, but I wanted an answer to the puzzle of how it was done that would be interesting and new. I'd originally planned to have Amanda be the guilty party, but sometimes characters just won't behave no matter how much I outline the plot! She insisted she was innocent and forced me to look for other suspects.

Thanks for spending time with Kate and Alex. Thanks again for spending time in my fictional world. I hope this book gave you a fun escape and an interesting puzzle.

As always, I hope you'll take a moment to post a short review where you purchased it. In this digital world, reviews play a big part in authors' lives. Not only do book buyers make decisions partly based on the number and quality of reviews, but advertisers use the same criteria to select books. A substantial number of honest reviews helps readers decide if the book is their cup of tea and also allows me to book advertising to reach new readers. If you want to support an author, post an honest review. Thanks in advance!

ABOUT THE AUTHOR

USA Today bestselling author Sara Rosett writes fun mysteries. Her books are light-hearted escapes for readers who enjoy atmospheric settings and puzzling mysteries. *Publishers Weekly* called Sara's books, "satisfying," "well-executed," and "sparkling."

Sara loves to get new stamps in her passport and considers dark chocolate a daily requirement. Find out more at Sara-Rosett.com.

Connect with Sara
www.SaraRosett.com

OTHER BOOKS BY SARA ROSETT

THIS IS SARA ROSETT'S COMPLETE library at the time of publication, but Sara has new books coming out all the time. Sign up for her newsletter to stay up to date on new releases.

High Society Lady Detective — 1920s country house mysteries

Murder at Archly Manor

Murder at Blackburn Hall

The Egyptian Antiquities Murder

Murder in Black Tie

An Old Money Murder in Mayfair

Murder on a Midnight Clear

Murder at the Mansions

Murder on Location — English village cozy mysteries

Death in the English Countryside

Death in an English Cottage

Death in a Stately Home

Death in an Elegant City

Menace at the Christmas Market (novella)

Death in an English Garden

Death at an English Wedding

On the Run — Travel, intrigue, and a dash of romance

Elusive

Secretive

Deceptive